*Robyn*

*35*

PENGUIN B

# CLOSED FOR WINTER

Georgia Blain was born in Sydney in 1964.
She has worked as a journalist and as a
copyright lawyer. *Closed for Winter* is her
first novel.

# GEORGIA BLAIN

# CLOSED FOR WINTER

PENGUIN BOOKS

Penguin Books Australia Ltd
487 Maroondah Highway, PO Box 257
Ringwood, Victoria 3134, Australia
Penguin Books Ltd
Harmondsworth, Middlesex, England
Viking Penguin, A Division of Penguin Books USA Inc.
375 Hudson Street, New York, New York 10014, USA
Penguin Books Canada Limited
10 Alcorn Avenue, Toronto, Ontario, Canada M4V 3B2
Penguin Books (NZ) Ltd
Cnr Rosedale and Airborne Roads, Albany, Auckland, New Zealand

First published by Penguin Books Australia Ltd 1998

1 3 5 7 9 10 8 6 4 2

Designed by Ellie Exarchos, Penguin Design Studio
Typeset in 11/15 pt Apollo MT by Post Pre-press Group, Brisbane
Made and printed in Australia by Australian Print Group, Maryborough, Victoria

National Library of Australia
Cataloguing-in-Publication data:

Blain, Georgia.
Closed for winter.

ISBN 0 14 027207 0.

I. Title.

A823.3

This project has been assisted by the Commonwealth Government through the
Australia Council, its arts funding and advisory body.

I would like to thank the Australian Society of Authors for the opportunity to take part in their mentorship scheme and Rosie Scott for being such a wonderful mentor.

I would also like to thank Louise, Tony, Catherine and Laura for advising me when I needed it.

Thank you also to Fiona Inglis and to Ali Watts and Julie Gibbs at Penguin for all their work in getting this book to its final stage.

And, finally, thank you to Anne and Andrew for their unwavering support and love.

# 1

Behind us the ocean is pale blue.

I hold the photograph up to the light and look closely. The colour has faded but I can remember it as it was. Silver-blue, but pink with the warmth of the last of the day.

We are silhouetted. Two young girls. Long limbed and gawky. Awkward, thin and misplaced. Me more so than Frances. At twelve, she stood poised on the edge of change and hating it. Furious with it and with everyone around her. But she had a certain grace, a certain strength in her defiance. You can see it, even in that picture.

At eight, I was still safely cocooned in childhood. Still on the right side of the fence. But I wanted to be like her. In the photo, I am trying to stand in the way that she stands. I am trying to look the way that she looks. But I am a child and she is not.

Our features? Eyes? Nose? Mouth? I hold the photograph closer but nothing is discernible. We are figures against a pale-blue backdrop. I cannot see the details, the parts that made up who we were. But if I close my eyes, if I concentrate, I can remember.

And it is the heat that I feel first.

Standing with my eyes closed in the house where I live with Martin, my photograph on the table in front of me.

Feeling the warmth of the sun on my shoulders as I lie in the rock pool again. Knowing that this is where I am because this is where I was every day of that summer.

And I am concentrating. I am taking myself back.

The row of shells on the rock ledge next to me, but they are not shells. They are my jewels. The seaweed on my back, but it is not seaweed. It is my hair. My legs stretched out in front of me, but they are not legs. They are my tail.

I remember.

I am a mermaid. Sliding down into the pool and holding my breath. Swimming down to my palace, deep down in the dark-blue sea.

This is the way I was.

And far off, the boys dive-bomb from the jetty. They run, full pelt, along the wooden planks and then leap, high in the air, legs tucked tight against the chest, shouting wildcat calls as they crash, like bullets, into the depths.

While outside this house, the house where I am now, the wind comes up from the gully, shaking the winter-wet branches of the trees, cold and bracing.

But I am not really here.

I am there.

In my pool, with my back to the jetty. Lost in my world; my sister, Frances, somewhere in hers. Up there on the jetty, leaning lazily against the railing, with the boys, a cigarette in one hand, her free arm draped around the waist of the toughest boy, the best-looking boy, a boy who also smokes a cigarette, pinched between his thumb and forefinger, down to the butt and then flicks it expertly into the ocean, where it floats bobbing on the surface.

This is what it was like. Day after day.

This is the place to which I try to return.

But it is not just this general picture that I am trying to remember. It is not just the summer as a whole. I am always trying to narrow it down. I am always trying to take myself back to the one day, to pick out the details that made that particular day what it was.

I turn the photograph over in my hands. On the reverse there is nothing, just the word 'Kodak' in pale-grey print. I have not written our names or the date on which the photo was taken. It was one of those days, but I do not know exactly which one.

No one knows I have this picture. Not even Dorothy, my mother. I have always kept it hidden and I change the hiding spot regularly. Or else I carry it around with me, tucked into the back of my diary. I bring it out when I am alone, when Martin is out and I am in the house by myself, when there is no one behind the box office desk with me, or on the bus after work.

I have had this photograph for years.

I have had it since that day.

And for months afterwards, I would keep it hidden under my pillow and each night I would take it out and stare at it, trying to take myself back, going through every detail to see if there was something I had missed, while at the other end of the house, my mother would be sitting in front of the television, chain-smoking in front of an endless blur of pictures, until, at last, she fell asleep.

I would hear her.

And then it would be quiet.

Silent.

I would turn off my light, close my eyes and tell myself, *Okay, one more time, from the beginning, in order,* and I would start again, picking through that day, piece by piece, from beginning to end.

And this is what I still do.

This is what I am trying to do now.

With my photograph under the light, I am taking myself back to that day.

*Tell us what happened?* they would ask when they questioned me later. And I would. Step by step. Over and over again.

*From the beginning.*

I would take myself back to that morning. I would see my mother getting ready for work, standing by the sink, a cup of coffee in one hand, a cigarette in the other, telling us what she always tells us. Frances is in charge. I must do as she says.

4

The sizzle of her cigarette as she butts it out in the sink. The pink lipstick on the rim of her coffee cup.

I start from here because this is where they would tell me to start. This is the logical place. *Tell us what happened?* they would ask. *From when your mother left*, they would say.

And I would hear her slam the door, late, shouting out instructions, running back to get her keys, her hair already loose and wild about her face.

And then gone.

Just Frances and I.

*And then?* they would ask, sometimes leaning forward, encouraging me to keep going, sometimes sitting back. Step by step. Over and over again.

And I would hear my sister telling me I have ten minutes and I know she is telling me I have to be ready by then, that she will go regardless of whether I am ready or not. It is up to me.

Step by step, through that day. Over and over again.

And I am racing to the bedroom, pushing past her. She is putting on her new bikini that she nicked from Grace Brothers last week. She is rubbing coconut oil into her legs. She is smearing gloss on her lips.

All of these details I can remember and recite.

*Wait*, I cry as she starts heading for the door, because I am still making my bed.

She has left hers as it is.

*Wait*, I shout again, knowing that she will not listen to me, knowing there is no time to smooth out the blankets and fold over the sheet in the way I like.

And I am running out the back door, into the glare of the day. I am chasing her, telling her to wait, seeing her there at the gate, pulling my towel off the line, pegs scattering behind me, as I run to catch up.

This is the way it was.

This is where I start because this is where they tell me to start.

But sometimes I want to go back. Further and further. Sometimes it doesn't feel right. Sometimes I just don't know. How can you understand one day without understanding the day before and the day before that one?

I have to stop myself. I have to pull myself back. Because otherwise it would be endless.

I have to begin at the beginning, from the place they tell me.

I have to remember.

# 2

Today is my twenty-eighth birthday. I am catching the
bus down to Dorothy's house. Martin will join us later
and I will cook dinner for the three of us. It was his idea.
Not hers and certainly not mine.

Martin and I live at one end of the number 12 bus
route, Dorothy lives at the other. From the foothills to the
beach. There is one road and it stretches, straight and
wide, no bends, no deviations, only the occasional slight
rise to alleviate the monotonous miles.

I know this road well. I have travelled it more times
than I could care to imagine.

When I was young, I caught this bus from my
mother's house to school. I would sit near the front,
where the adults sat, not wanting to hear the others
down the back, and hoping they would not notice me.
But they were impossible to ignore.

The old man sitting next to me would tut-tut and

shake his head in disapproval as a school bag came spinning up the aisle.

*You're dead, mate,* and there would be a scuffle and a thump as someone hit the floor.

The girls would laugh, blowing perfect streams of smoke into the air, and the bus driver would pull over to the side of the road.

*Okay*, he would shout, *you and you — out*.

Not one of them would move.

*You heard me*, and he would glare at them, one more time, before finally giving up with a shrug of his shoulders.

And the bus would groan as he veered it back into the morning traffic.

I caught this bus into the city when I studied Business at the Institute of Technology. Lectures five days a week for three years, and I would go in on the number 12 in the morning and home on the number 12 in the early afternoon. When I finished studying, I started working at the State Theatre, and I still caught the number 12. From Dorothy's to my job.

Now that I live with Martin, I just catch it from the other direction, from Martin's house to work, and, once a week, from work to Dorothy's and from Dorothy's back to Martin's, travelling the entire route, from the sea to the newly planted eucalypts in our suburb.

So, I know this road well.

I know the progression of houses, from the neat brick homes where Martin and I live to the cluster of office blocks in the city, to the sprawl of low houses that get shabbier as you get closer to the beach.

I know each brick fence, each gravel drive and each front door.

I know the shops, the small supermarkets, the milk bars selling hamburgers and the video stores. A group on every third or fourth corner, and the occasional one on its own, a furniture shop or a hardware store that struggles to stay open, because no one stops along this straight wide road any more.

*When we get the insurance money, we will move to a place like that,* Dorothy used to say pointing to one of the new brick houses closer to the city. She would squeeze our hands. *Your father loved me and he will have made sure that we are all right.* She would toss her hair back and her voice would become louder and louder. *He loved me and I loved him.*

Everyone on the bus could hear. We could feel their eyes on us and we kept ours fixed on the ground. Staring at our feet. Waiting to see who would kick first. The tap of my sister's toe against my heel, the knock of my own shoe against hers, back and forth, back and forth, in time to the relentless flow of our mother's words.

When the insurance money finally did come, it was only just enough to buy the house that we lived in, the house that I grew up in, the house that I did not leave until I was twenty-two.

I have never wanted one of those new brick houses. But I live in one now. With Martin. His mother left it to him when she died.

On our third night out together, he took me back to his house and when he opened the front door, I noticed the smell. It was like everything had been covered in plastic. I stood at the entrance, hesitant to go in.

*This is it*, Martin said proudly as he turned on the hall light, and I remember wishing he hadn't said that. *This is it*. This was the escape that I was choosing.

I sat nervously in the lounge room while he made me a cup of tea. It was like sitting in a waiting room. Out of the corner of my eye, I could see a photo on his desk. I picked it up and held it under the light. It was a wedding photo.

*My wife*, Martin said, when he brought the tea in.

I was embarrassed at being caught, and in my rush to put it back where I found it, I dropped it.

*I should have told you*, he said. *She left me*, he explained, *about four months ago*, and when he looked up from the floor where the photograph lay at our feet, I accidently brushed his hand.

*It's all right*, he said, *we weren't suited*.

I looked down at his wife's face, there in her white dress on the shag pile in his mother's house, and I could feel the pressure of his hand in mine.

Everything was quiet.

Outside, the evening wind from the gully was making the gum trees sway and bend, silver against the night sky, leaves shaking in a mass, and I closed my eyes and imagined I had slammed his front door behind me and run up those streets, up past the last line of houses to the blackness of the hills beyond. Running as I run in my dreams, tireless for miles, until from somewhere high above, I looked down on all this. All the lights of the houses, sparkling small and insignificant, and in the midst of them, this house, with him and me sitting here in this room, in this silence.

I did not lift my gaze to meet his. It was him. He lifted my head in his hands until my mouth met his, and he kissed me. Briefly.

*I will show you the bathroom*, he said.

And I followed him, silent, thinking, *This is it. This is it.*

Outside it is night. In winter, it gets dark early, and by the time I leave work, the day has gone. When I look out the bus window, I can only see the lights of the houses and the cars. I lean my head against the cold glass and feel the chill against my skin.

By the time we reach my stop, the bus is empty. It is the second-last stop on the route. Martin's house is the second-last stop at the other end of the route. I pull the cord, and the bus driver brakes suddenly.

*Sorry,* he says, *I thought everyone had already got off.*

I can only just hear his voice above the shudder of the engine as he pulls up to the side of the road. But I think that was what he said to me.

The wind is blowing off the sea and there is salt in the air. I can taste it on the tip of my tongue. My coat flies behind me as I walk down the road to the small group of shops at the back of Dorothy's house.

Every week I shop for her. John Mills, the doctor who lives up the street, also shops for her. He buys what she needs. I buy the things that she does not want him to know about. She leaves a list on the table for me, near the door, so that I will pick it up when I leave. Without anything ever needing to be said.

I buy her cigarettes at the newsagency and her beer at the bottle shop next door. I also buy food for our dinner tonight; steak, potatoes and peas, and, at the last minute, a cake from the supermarket because it is, after all, my birthday.

As I am coming out of the shop, I see Mrs Donovan. I try to look away, but it is too late. Our eyes meet.

*Hello, Elise.* She smiles and her voice has a measure of concern. They are all like this. They will always be like this. *How's your poor mother?* she asks.

I tell her that she's fine and as I speak, I turn my whole body away from her, wanting to look like I am in a hurry.

*You know if ever there's anything you need done, you just have to ask.*

I am not sure what she means but I smile politely and thank her.

*I'm sure Jo-anne would love to catch up. Maybe you could come and have dinner next time she visits? Or I could arrange an evening?*

Jo-anne is her daughter. We went to school together but we were not friends.

Mrs Donovan is not really concerned for me. She is just curious. They are all just curious. Still. After all these years.

I tell her that I must hurry. I turn my back on her as I am saying goodbye because I do not want to see that look on her face.

On Military Road the wind is wild. It comes straight off the ocean. I can feel the spray from the sea even though I am two streets back, and above my head the pine trees creak dangerously. The streetlights are out and I walk quickly, head down, forcing my way through the gust. There are not many cars. One comes towards me, crawling slowly, and I can hear the bass of the stereo speakers long before it gets close. As it passes, the driver leans on his horn, and someone winds down the window and shouts out to me. I cannot hear the words above the music and the roar of the wind. It may be someone I know. It may not.

I just keep my head low and walk faster.

I hate these streets at night.

# 3

You often do not see things until you are forced to see them through the eyes of someone else.

That is the way it is for me.

I do not think I ever really saw our house until Martin first came here. I do not think I ever really saw Dorothy either. But perhaps I did. Somewhere, deep inside. I just did not want to admit it to myself.

This is the house that my mother came to when she married Franco. Thirty-two years ago. Eighteen and pregnant, with her wide, startled eyes and her thick auburn hair. My mother was beautiful. This is what she has told me. Often.

*I had the most beautiful legs*, and she would pull her dress up high, right there on the street. Frances would ignore her. I would blush scarlet. She would keep on talking. *But now look at them. This is what happens when you are left on your own with two children.* And she would sigh, then drop all her bags on the pavement, so that she could truly sigh, with no distractions. *He loved me this much.* She would stretch her arms out wide. *He really loved me.* She would sigh one more time and then she would pick up the shopping with one last sigh to signal that the performance was over. It was our cue to start walking again.

But a few steps further on, she would start again. Her litany was endless.

*We had nothing but our love for each other*, she would tell us. *We did not even own this house. Your father had to go off and earn money. As soon as we were married.*

And he had. Miles away. A linesman with the electricity trust in the far north.

*It broke his heart, to be away. Because he loved me. This much.* And her arms were outstretched again, graceful like the ballerina she had dreamed of being.

*This much,* Frances would mock, rolling her eyes in disgust. *This bloody much.*

*Don't,* I would say, but she would not stop.

*This much, this much, this much*, as she would dance around the room, and I would watch her, terrified of Dorothy walking through the bedroom door and witnessing Frances's mockery and my own guilty laughter. *This much*, and she would pull me up from where I sat on my bed and twirl me round, both of us giggling now, her skirt up high, both of us laughing, twirling and twirling, until we collapsed, dizzy, exhausted, on the bed.

*This much*, we would whisper, one more time, in unison. *This much.*

15

And then Frances would turn away from me.

*This much*, I would say, hopefully.

But she would not respond.

*This much*, I would try again. Wanting her back. Reaching for her. My words faint in the silence that had descended.

But the game was over. As suddenly as it had begun.

My mother is fifty now. It is not old, but she seems old. She is no longer the wild girl who danced too much, talked too much and drank too much.

*All the boys were in love with me*, she would say, looking at herself in the mirror. *The girls did not like me, they were envious, but the boys . . .*

I can see her now as she would have been then. Never still, never silent, eager, laughing too loudly as one of them put his hands on her hips and another stroked her thigh. And I can see the other girls, sipping their shandies and watching with tight-lipped disapproval, whispering behind her back and shaking their heads, *She is so embarrassing.*

*They were envious*, my mother would repeat.

Perhaps they were. But now they are just curious, thinly veiled by a sad-eyed, 'we knew this would happen' concern. *Poor thing*, they say to each other, and they look at me, worried and anxious, including me in their circle of righteousness as an act of charity.

But my mother is oblivious to them. This house is now her world. She does not see them and she does not hear them. She probably never did.

She spends most days sitting at the kitchen table,

writing letters or clipping newspaper articles and arranging them into two neat piles: 'Similar Stories' and 'Possibilities'. She pastes these into scrapbooks. There are a pile of them in my old bedroom. She does not look at them again, but she needs to know they are there. They may contain that clue, that link she needs should she ever come close to unravelling the whole story. Because I think she still believes that one day she will find out what happened. I think she still believes that one day she will know.

So, when I arrive at the back door, she is there at the table. She is always there. In the yellow of the fluorescent light, she reads and pastes and reads and pastes. When I leave her, she goes back to her seat and continues, while outside the winter winds numb the hands of the old men on the jetty. Fishing for sharks in the midnight ocean.

This is my mother.

I never really saw her until I was forced to see her through the eyes of someone else. She never really sees me, and she never will. She looks at me through a cloud. The few words I say are like branches scratching on the windowpanes. Irritating, but they do not touch her. They just beat on the thick glass that protects her.

When Martin first came here, I was forced to see her as she is, and to see what this house had become. But perhaps I already had, and that was why I never wanted him to visit.

Or perhaps I did not want to see him.

He came to the front, although I had told him not to. We have always come in the back way. The front door was stuck from years of wet winters and long dry summers. I pulled and he pushed but it would not move.

*Come round the back*, I kept on telling him. But he did not listen.

*Jesus*, he said when he finally burst through, the whole house shuddering with the force of his impact, *you need to do something about that*.

And as he stood there, hot and sweaty in the dark corridor, I saw the rips in the carpet and the dim yellowing paint on the walls, fibro walls that sagged like cardboard in the wet and dried again in the intense heat of summer, powdery dry. And I saw him in his neat jeans and ironed shirt with button-down collar, his face pink and shiny from the effort.

*I'll just get my things*, I said, hoping he would stay where he was, but he didn't. He was right behind me. Through the lounge room and past the photograph of Frances.

*Who's that?* he asked.

I told him it was my sister, but as I spoke, I kept on walking, out to the kitchen, with him right on my heels.

She was there, sitting at the table, watching us both as we came in.

Dorothy.

He held out his hand, but she did not move. She just looked at him. Up and down. I did not want to see what she saw.

*Pleased to meet you*, and Martin pulled out a chair and sat down opposite her. *I think I just about succeeded in knocking the house down.*

She turned back to her papers.

She continued reading.

*Anything interesting in the news?* he asked.

*Not yet,* and she did not lift her gaze.

I could feel my fingers pressing into my arms, white, and I willed him, with all my concentration, to notice that I wanted to go.

*Shall we have a cup of tea?* he suggested, thinking that the two words he had managed to drag out of her were an indication that she was coming around. *There's no rush, is there?* and he looked up at me, standing silent by the kitchen sink.

Dorothy put her scissors down.

*I am quite busy,* she said, in the pompous voice she uses when she is irritated. *I have a lot to get through,* and she indicated the pile of papers in front of her.

I was looking directly at Martin now, waiting for him to meet my eye, waiting for him to understand. And at last he pushed his chair back, the leg lifting a corner of the lino. He flattened it back down again.

*She's a little dotty, isn't she?* he said as we headed out the back gate, and he reached to put his arm around my shoulder.

I had already moved away.

The three of us are in the kitchen now. I am cooking my birthday dinner and Martin is talking loudly about work. I do not listen. I concentrate on pounding the steak until it is tender. Dorothy does not listen either. She turns the pages of the paper slowly.

Outside the wind howls. It blows in through the crack

under the door and lifts the carpets in the hall. If I stepped out there now, it would be billowing, like the ocean, beneath my feet. Martin once offered to tack it down for her but Dorothy told him there was no need. She liked it as it was.

*Your father always enjoyed a steak,* she says as I drop each piece into the pan. She speaks above Martin until he is forced to be silent. *When he would come back from work, tired and hungry, I would cook it for him.*

It is likely that she is lying. I cannot remember Dorothy ever cooking for him. But perhaps she did, back then, when he was alive. I cannot remember.

Martin clears the table. He reaches for the pile of Dorothy's papers but she stops him.

*These are not read*, she says, and she moves them herself to a stack in the corner of the kitchen.

Martin offers us all a glass of wine. Dorothy only drinks beer and I do not want one, but he pours three glasses anyway.

It is one of his favourites. *An excellent year*, and he sniffs his glass appreciatively.

He passes one to Dorothy but she ignores him.

*I have a present for you,* she says, and I am surprised she has remembered, even more surprised that she has made some effort towards celebrating the occasion.

She goes off to her bedroom and comes back with a bundle of brown paper tied together with one of my old hair ribbons.

I am anxious as I take it from her. Martin leans over my shoulder and I can sense his amused curiosity. He is

20

wondering what Dotty Dot, as he likes to call her, has got for me.

To most eyes, it would seem to be just an old piece of material. Pale-blue and dirty. But I can feel how slippery cool it is beneath my fingers and as I lift its weightlessness from the paper, I know what it is. As a child I had loved it. A wedding gift she had bought for herself. A satin dressing-gown. I remember how beautiful she had looked as she had spun around the living room in it.

And as I smile at her, she smiles back. It is just a moment, a brief instant, but it is enough to make me glad to have come here after all.

*Thank you,* I say and I can see Dorothy is pleased I am pleased.

Martin leans over my shoulder. *I'm looking forward to seeing you in that,* he laughs.

That night, we drive home in silence. The windows have fogged in the rain and Martin swears as he leans forward to wipe a small circle of vision in the windscreen. The heater is on full and there is no air. I am concentrating on pushing down the nausea.

*Well, that wasn't so bad,* he says, referring to the evening.

His voice jolts in the quiet. I do not answer him.

He turns on the radio and starts humming to the music.

*Although God knows what she intended by giving you that filthy rag.* He takes my hand and squeezes it in his own. There is concern in his voice now and I do not want to hear what he has started to say. *I think we're going to*

21

*have to talk again*, he says, gently, *about the possibility of a home*.

I stare out the window.

*Not tonight*, he says, patting my fingers, *but soon*.

I stare at the patterns the rain is making on the glass and I think to myself that I will not even bother to turn around and fight him. He is a fool to think that he could make her leave that house. He has no idea.

*Don't sulk*, he says, when we pull into the driveway.

*Why the silent treatment?* he asks as I brush my teeth.

*You're impossible*, he says, finally giving up on me, and he shrugs his shoulders as he turns towards the bedroom.

I want to be by myself.

In the kitchen, I take my photo out from under the lining of the cutlery drawer. And, holding it up to the light, I try to see us as we really were.

# 4

Even this early in the morning it is hot. Everything is still, stunned and helpless in the relentless shimmer. The labrador from across the road has surrendered. She lies, tongue hanging out, in the shade of the scrappy almond tree by the fence. Underfoot, the asphalt seems to melt, black sticky tar, sweet smelling and soft to the tread.

Frances leads. I follow. There are no other people on the street and it is quiet, weekday quiet, with the desolation that descends once the working day has begun. Mothers who stay at home stay inside with the blinds down and the doors shut. They know what today will be like, and there is no sign of possible relief in the sky. No wisp of cloud, no faint breath of wind, no hint of change.

I walk at least ten feet behind, watching Frances ahead of me, the swing of the narrow hips, the long-legged stride, and I wish I could be like that. I do not dare run up alongside her. I have been forbidden. She may be my friend at home but outside it is a different matter, and I obey her orders. Without question.

Across Military Road and to the other side, we pass the Brownswords', and I look in, hoping Tamara will be out the front and allowed to come to the beach with us. But the yard is empty, and the front door closed. Even if she had been there, it is unlikely Mrs Brownsword would have agreed. Frances is not responsible enough, in fact she is *A bad influence*. I know. I have heard it whispered, even spoken aloud in my presence, and I blush each time, ashamed and angry at my inability to defend my sister.

Down Grange Road, the last stretch which is not so bleak as the rest, and at the end, over a slight rise, there is The Esplanade, stretching for miles, and beyond that the sea.

Frances crosses the road and stands, the jetty and the kiosk to her left, waiting for me to catch up. This is where we always confer, briefly, quickly, not long enough for any of Frances's friends to see us together. Although it is unlikely that any of them will be here yet. Frances likes to come early, to sunbake before they arrive so her dark tan will seem effortless, like all her attributes, and not something she has had to work on. Like the way she smokes, practised in secret, drawback perfected, before she made it public, or the lazy flick of her hair, blow-dried at home to look like it just did that, by itself. I know this but I say nothing because I, too, admire. I watch and I learn because I want to be like that. To look like I don't care. One day.

24

This is the plan. I will stay near the shallow pools to the right of the jetty. I will not swim unless Frances is there to watch me. I must not bother Frances under any circumstances. Frances will come and get me at lunchtime.

But –

Frances looks at me impatiently. What question could there be?

I close my mouth and wait, squinting in the glare, for her to turn and walk ahead, along the wooden planking that leads down through the white-hot sand and the dry grasses to the beach. I will follow at a discreet distance and at the end of the path, I will turn to the right, Frances to the left.

This is what happened. On that day and on every other day. There were no differences, no changes to a routine we had followed each morning of that summer. I think I am certain of that. But when they questioned me afterwards, my certainty was shaken. I knew that all they wanted was to hear that I had noticed a difference. Any crumb, any scrap, anything tangible to pick up and examine. And I would try again, winding it back to the beginning so that I could retrace each step until I was standing on the wooden planking again, watching Frances disappear down that path, striding off past the jetty to her favourite spot where she would be hidden, nestled between two pillows of burning white sand.

*But did you actually see her there?*

It is high tide, and the pools are full. There is no swell. There is never any swell at these beaches. Just the gentle roll of the sea to the shore.

Once, years ago, I went to the surf. In a tiny hot car, Frances and I in the back seat, our mother in the front. We had driven for miles, to the country. To rolling hills the colour of wheat, and beyond that the ocean.

*This is fun,* Dorothy had laughed, and she had run to where the surf crashed in a white fury on the shore. Frances had followed. Screaming as she dived in and was thrown under and up and out again, her long hair a tangle of sand and seaweed.

I had stayed on the shore and watched. Too frightened. Even when Dorothy had bent down low, arms out, to coax me to the edge, just the edge, I had hung back.

*Scaredy cat. Scaredy, scaredy, scaredy cat,* Frances had sung, round and round in circles, Dorothy laughing, eventually scooping me up in her arms and taking me in, held safe, high above the waves, but still screaming. Screaming blue murder in the blue blue sea.

So, I like it here. Here where it is safe in the pools. When I lower myself in, the water comes just to my waist. No further. And it is cool. I do not like the heat and the sand, I do not like the flies, and this place is my own. Just mine.

On the jetty, an old woman eats fish and chips. Wrapped in newspaper. She breaks off fragments of the batter with her fingernails and tosses them across the wooden boards to the gulls gathered at her feet. They squawk furiously, pecking each other in the race for scraps. And then, standing at the railing, she throws the remains over the edge. The gulls dive and swoop in an angry whirl of grey, and the noise is, for one instant, deafening.

26

I look up, startled by the cry of the birds. Out on the edge of the jetty, I see the boys gathering in a small group, tight black jeans and no shirts. They egg each other on, push each other, jostle each other, until one will eventually take the plunge. The first jump of the day. A dive-bomb that will rupture the smooth surface of the ocean, and down he will plummet, and then up again, glittering in the dazzle of sunlight as he pulls himself back up the ladder, wet jeans clinging to long thin legs.

Under the jetty, families spread out towels in the cool. Eskies, cricket bats, li-los, books that are dog-eared at the corners; they are setting themselves up for the day. I watch. A dog snaps at the ankle of a girl who walks too close, a baby starts crying, a father slaps his son. A brother and sister fight and one of them runs off to tell, *You'll be sorry*, while the other stays behind, hiding behind the pylons, and I drift in and drift out, sometimes aware, sometimes sensing no more than a general blur in the background.

*But did you see anything? Anything at all that was even a little bit unusual?*

I cannot think. I cannot pinpoint that moment they are looking for.

I look up from my pool and try to find my sister. Just occasionally. To know where she is. To the left of the jetty are the dunes. Not really dunes, just gentle mounds of sand. She is normally there for most of the morning. Out of sight. Any clear vision is blocked by the pylons and then the sand itself. I scan along the shoreline but I know it is unlikely Frances will be in the water.

I do not panic. It is just a routine check. And I slide back into the cool blue, deep down, bubbling a lungful of air back up to the surface and then out again, my hair a long wet snake down my back.

The sun climbs higher, until it is a flat white disc burning a hole in the sky. Lunches are bought from the kiosk, or unpacked from baskets. Sandwiches, hot chips, chicken, pies; I can smell it all and I am hungry. I want to go home, and I stand, no longer a mermaid, but unsteady on my legs, to look for Frances. To look across to the dunes, to the water, to the end of the jetty and behind me, to the path leading up to the road. And then again, fingers crossed, hopeful that this time I will see her.

But there is nothing.

Only families and children and the boys on the jetty and the sand and the ocean, and no Frances.

So I sit in the pool again. And wait. I do not want to move, because I had promised I would be here. If I move we might miss each other. Frances may come back and walk home without me. And I would be left alone on the beach. Waiting and waiting for something that had already gone.


The storm has stopped and everything is still.

The only sound is the hum of the refrigerator in the corner and the ticking of the kitchen clock. These streets are quiet. Suburban backstreets. Everyone sleeps at night and everyone works during the day.

I pull the cutlery drawer out to put my photograph

away, and the knives and forks rattle. I wait nervously for Martin to call out to me. Nothing.

He, too, is asleep. Snoring in his flannel pyjamas. Content without me and oblivious to the fact that I am angry with him.

I pull back the quilt on my side of the bed and Martin does not wake.

My side of the bed. I lie narrow and straight so that I will not touch him. My eyes are closed but I am not asleep. I am willing him to wake and open his arms to me. I want him to open his arms to me.

He does not move.

If he did, I would only pull away. This is what happens between us.

Over and over again.

So, I lie there, with him and alone, and far away, underneath the jetty, the water slaps against the pylons, bleached and coated with barnacles.

# 5

*This cannot go on.*

These are Martin's last words to me as he leaves in the morning. He is referring to my silence. I can see that he is confused, that he does not understand. I can also see that he is fed up.

I do not want to speak to him until he apologises. But how can I explain that when I am not talking to him? And I do not even know what apology it is that I want. I fear it is so large it amounts to no less than apologising for his very existence.

I do not want him. But I do not want him to leave me. And I am terrified that I am driving him away.

Martin and I both work at the State Theatre. He is the financial controller and I am the box office manager. This was how we met, seven years ago.

When I started at the theatre, I did not want anyone to know who I was.

Throughout my school years, I lived with the knowledge that they knew, all of them, what had happened. I was her sister. That was my identity and I could not escape it. I was as quiet as I could possibly be, unobtrusive and unnoticeable in the hope that they would soon forget I existed, and that it had happened.

But it did not work.

Head down, eyes to the ground, I would walk past the boys behind the bike shed, older boys who had known her, and I would feel their gaze, the sting of their curiosity. My cheeks would burn.

Outside the tuckshop, the girls would look me up and down, their whispers scratching the air around me. Like nettles. Her friends or her enemies? I did not know. I drew circles around them all. Zones of danger. Areas to avoid.

And it was not just those who had known her. Even those who hadn't had heard. *That's her. Poor little thing*. The mothers who waited at the gate would watch me when I came out at home time. The teachers would monitor me with concern. The children in my year avoided me as if I were contaminated.

They all knew.

I was marked and I had no escape. Not in that school and not in the next.

The first day of Marketing at the Institute of Technology, I stood up shyly and tried to do what I had been asked. To market myself. To introduce myself to the class. I am shy now, but then it was even worse. It had no limits. I had been waiting for my turn, faint with dread.

31

I had been unable to bear the thought of having to explain who I was. I had been trying to prepare something to say, but when my moment came, all that I had prepared slipped like water through my fingers.

And I lied.

Apart from my name, there was not a word of truth in all I said.

I headed back to my place, giddy and light with what I had done.

But then I heard it.

*Oh yeah?* someone hissed as I sat down. I looked around and saw him. Eyes staring straight at me. It was one of them. One of the boys from school. And I felt a fool for having imagined there was a possibility of escape.

But at the State Theatre Company, no one knew me. I applied for the position by filling out a form. Just the bare details. In the interview I gave nothing away. It was not difficult, I was experienced by then. And as I answered their questions, I knew I had finally succeeded in hiding it all; locked it up, put it away, out of reach from everyone.

I had become what I had tried to be. Unobtrusive. Unnoticeable.

I look at my reflection in the mirror as I get ready for work and it seems there is no definition to my face. There are no lines to mark where I end and the air begins. But this is a bad day, I tell myself. This is not all there is. It cannot be. I lean forward anxiously until my forehead hits the glass, and I pull back, a dull throb in my head. I feel like a fool.

Martin is the only one who knows the story. He is the only one who knows who I am.

*I didn't know you had a sister,* he had said, referring to the photograph he had seen in our living room. I had forgotten about it in my relief that we had finally left Dorothy in the kitchen. The first visit was over. He had seen. I would not have to show him again.

But there was that photograph.

We were driving south, inching our way through the miles of outer suburbs that eventually lead to the periphery of this city. It was hot, the dry heat of a desert town, and the wind blew gritty, its mounting fury swinging the awnings on used-car yards and petrol stations. It would catch at your throat and make your eyes sting. I could see it and I could imagine it. But I could not feel it.

Martin turned the airconditioning up another notch.

There were goosebumps on my arms.

*Is she older than you?*

He put his foot down on the accelerator in an attempt to overtake the car in front. There was a truck coming towards us. I closed my eyes. He swore loudly as he was forced to pull back into the lane we had just left.

He was taking me away for the weekend, to stay with friends of his whom I had never met.

*She's a painter and he's a writer*, he had said, proud of his links to the artistic world.

He had described them and I had imagined them. They had made me nervous before I had even met them, and I had tried to make excuses, reasons why I had to stay at home, but it had been futile.

*Please,* I had eventually said, *I am no good with strangers. You will have a better time on your own.*

He had looked at me with disbelief. If it came to going on his own, he would rather stay at home. *The reason why I am with you is so that I have someone to do things with. So that I do not have to be on my own*, he had said.

And when I had protested again, he had told me that I was adorable and that he would look after me. He had circled me in his arms, so tight that I could not breathe, and I had given in, terrified at the prospect of what I was about to encounter, terrified that I would spend the entire weekend silent.

He pulled up at a petrol station and opened his door, letting in a blast of hot air. *Okay,* I told myself, *when he gets back in, I will tell him everything.* I prepared myself, the whole story ready to be laid out in front of him, and as he turned the key in the ignition, I was about to begin. But he spoke first.

*You'll love this place*, he said, *and Marissa's paintings. Not my kind of thing, but they'll be worth a lot one day. Mark my words*, and as he pulled out of the service station, he told me he had always been interested in the art market. He had a theory, he said, about how you could make money.

*Simple really*, and he began to explain it to me. In detail.

The moment was gone.

I had not told my story. I had not said what I wanted to say. And so I was left, waiting for him to bring up my sister again and knowing that when he did, I still had to speak. All weekend I dreaded the moment when he would ask. The few words that I managed came out heavy and solid; I could only just squeeze them past the bulk of all that was still unsaid.

On our last night, I heard Marissa whisper to Robert as I tiptoed past their bedroom to our own. *He never shuts up, and she never says a word.*

*Shhh,* he answered, *they'll hear.*

I had spent the afternoon with her, picking figs and apricots in a garden that tumbled down the hill to the sea, brilliant in the distance. I had wanted to tell her that I had always longed for a garden like this, I had wanted to compare it with the place from where I had come, but when I began, Martin interrupted.

*Poor Elise grew up with a pebbled back yard*, he laughed. *I don't think she'd seen a flower until she moved in with me.*

I said nothing.

Later, when I asked her how she knew Martin, she told me that she didn't. Not really. She had known his wife.

It was not until that night, our last night, that I finally told Martin. Unable to bear it any longer, I told him the whole story, all that I could remember, while outside, the branches of the olive trees swayed dark against the window.

But it was not the story I had prepared for him in the car. It was a story I had not spoken out loud, and with my first attempt to voice it, it came out tangled and twisted, falling in a heap between us.

I do not know what reaction I had expected.

He sat up in bed. It was, he said, extraordinary. Impossible. There must be a way we could work out what had happened to her. If we went over every detail, wrote a list. Still drunk from dinner, he became excited. He put forward possibility after possibility, certain each time that he had found the answer, the answer that no one had managed to find before him.

*No,* I said, wanting to retract it all. *That is not the point.*

How could I explain? I hadn't told him because I wanted him to solve it. I had told him because I wanted him to understand. I wanted him to know.

And I wanted him to care.

But he did not listen. He just kept on talking until eventually he saw my face and he realised he had gone wrong.

*Please,* I said. *Don't tell.*

And he promised. Did not question me as he normally would, but solemnly swore he would stay quiet. My secret was safe.

As far as I know, he is still the only one who knows.

To the others I am just Elise Silverton.

Unobtrusive and unnoticeable.

# 6

Newspapers, like photographs, deteriorate with age. The paper yellows and becomes brittle, fragile to the touch. The print remains, stamped black on the page, but the page eventually crumbles in the fingers, like ash.

The first article, the one that announced our story to the world, is pasted at the front of Dorothy's first scrapbook. It is brief and matter-of-fact: the date, the time and our names. At the top there is a copy of the photograph that is in our living room. Frances, aged eleven. Frances in her school uniform smiling at the camera. It does not look like her, but it was the only photograph my mother had.

The article is dated Monday 10 January 1974. It appeared in a newspaper that no longer exists. The paper was once the colour of the page on which it is pasted. There is now a contrast. It has aged more rapidly than her book.

My photograph has also deteriorated. The corners are

bent and creased and there are fingermarks across the print from where I have held it. There is a stain on the back, coffee-coloured, and the colours of the image are no longer true.

Dorothy keeps photocopies of that first newspaper article, a pile of them in a folder on the kitchen table. She puts a copy in each letter that she writes. I know. I have seen her.

She writes her letters in the morning. Long letters to people she does not know. She reads their stories in the paper and then clips the article for her 'Similar Stories' book. She has their names and then she finds their addresses, sometimes just from the phone book, sometimes she has to be more resourceful.

*Dear Jeanne (may I call you Jeanne?),*

*My name is Dorothy and I too have been through a similar experience to what you are now experiencing. I am writing to you because I thought it might help to hear from someone who knows how you feel. And believe me, none of them (the police, your friends, even the rest of your family) really know . . .*

She does not write these letters quickly. Sometimes they take her days. She will sit at the table, staring out past the sink to the window, her eyes narrowed in concentration. She is taking the few scraps of information she has from the newspaper article and trying to become that person. She wants to see what they see and to feel what they feel. Only then will she start writing again.

I know. I have watched her. It is like watching some-one disappear.

When she finishes, she signs her letters with her full name, *Dorothy Elise Silverton*. I have read them late at night while she sleeps and I have wondered who this person is. I have tried to soak up the words on the page, pretending that she was speaking them out loud to me and not just writing them to a stranger.

I have never told her that I know this other side to her.

I have never told Martin that she is not just what she appears to be. Dotty Dot, whose life has become confined to this house he feels she should leave. Mad Dorothy bab-bling forth a stream of stories, the layers of truth and imaginings tangled in and out of each other, or abruptly lapsing into a silence that may last for hours. It is always one or the other, never the in between, never the con-versation of a person who listens and responds.

Except in those letters.

She finishes writing at midday. There is a knock on the door and she stops. Puts her pen away, gathers up her papers and lets him in. John Mills, standing on the cracked cement steps, one hand clutching a white paper bag and the other resting on the rusted handle of the fly-screen door.

He brings ham and tomato sandwiches. Always. One for each of them, and when I was at home, sick from school or studying, one for me too.

They eat in the kitchen. She makes coffee, strong and black, *The way your father liked it,* and she smokes a cig-arette while they drink it. He frowns with disapproval.

*When I was young, I was the only girl who could blow smoke rings,* and she blows three, expertly. *I was also the only girl who could drink with the boys and not be sick. I could run faster than any of them, stay out later and dance until dawn. I have a constitution to envy. Besides,* and she smiles at him, *I only ever have one a day now. No one will buy them for me when they do the shopping.*

I have sat in the corridor and listened to them talk. He does not laugh at her wild and impossible stories. He does not try to silence her.

He was once her doctor but he is now retired. Strictly speaking, his visits are no longer professional. They have not been for a long time. But despite the fact that his surgery is now closed, he still likes to do his rounds. Just a few of his old patients. People whom he visits regularly; my mother the most regularly of all.

*Loneliness is the worst illness of all,* he once said.

And I did not know whether he was referring to his patients or to himself.

He spends most mornings working on a mosaic in his garden. It is the image of his wife, who is dead. I have never seen it, but I have heard him describe it to Dorothy. Sometimes he will bring tiles to show her.

*The colour of her lips*, he will say, and he will lay dark china-red on the table. *Her eyes,* and the blue will glitter like the icy tips of winter waves. *Her hair*, and it gleams, deep dark gold.

He works from a photograph. A picture of his wife as a young woman. When he showed me, I was surprised. Her hair was brown and her eyes were hazel.

40

*It's called artistic licence,* he laughed when I pointed it out to him.

I was young and I did not know what he meant.

He washes up before he leaves, checks that there is nothing else she needs, and then he is gone, leaving Dorothy alone.

In the early afternoon the kitchen is cool. The sun has moved to the front of the house. In summer this is a relief, in winter it is cold and she lights the gas heater, the blue flame hissing and flickering by her feet.

This is the time for her clippings.

She sits, oblivious to the day slowly folding into night, and reads until she is surprised to find herself with just the light from the heater illuminating the room. I know. I have come home to find her hunched over the paper in the dark. I have flicked on the fluoro light and seen her startled, stunned by its sudden brightness, because in her search, she has lost all awareness of the world that surrounds her.

Dotty Dot.

Martin sees the surface only. This is the way he is. And it is not just with her.

He looks at me and I doubt that he can hear or see all that I do not say or show.

There is a fear inside me. I hold my photograph up to the light and I try to see more clearly. I, too, become lost in my search. This is my flipside. Dorothy's letters are hers.

Sometimes I think we are just reverse sides of the same coin.

# 7

I am late for work.

It is not like me and when I arrive, I can see that Jocelyn is anxious.

I am also anxious. All morning it has been difficult to do anything.

*This cannot go on.*

I know that Martin is right but I cannot see a way to alter what we have become. We have walked too far down the wrong path. In moments of honesty, I have to admit to myself that we have never been on the right path.

But Martin is not my only anxiety.

This morning as I soaked Dorothy's blue satin nightgown in the laundry, I found myself staring out across Martin's neat square of lawn and native shrubs. I remembered how I had once wanted to plant vegetables and flowers and I could not remember how and when I had finally given up on the idea. I saw the pebbles in my mother's back garden. I saw that house, and I saw her. I had left her to come to this. This had been my escape, but the thought of her eats at me. Constantly.

Jocelyn asks me if everything is all right.

*Fine,* I tell her, unable to speak the truth.

Jocelyn and I have worked together for seven years. For her, and for most of the other people who work on the box office, this is just a job for money. She is a sculptor.

*I would like to do you,* she had once said. She had been showing me her work. Most of them were nudes. *You have such a beautiful body.*

I had not known how to respond.

Later, when I told Martin, he teased me. *She's probably trying to crack on to you,* he laughed, nudge, nudge. *Better not wear those short skirts to work any more.*

I did not speak to him of it again.

But I did model for Jocelyn. When she asked me the second time, I agreed.

I sat for her for six months, once a week. When we finished work, we would go to her kitchen and drink beer. She would show me books from art school and we would talk about what we liked and what we didn't like.

I never told her a lot about myself, but I told her more than I have told other people, sometimes surprising myself with what I would reveal.

I know that Jocelyn does not like Martin. She would not tell me that now but she used to, when I first started working here. She would make faces behind his back when he came to check on how the 'box office girls' were doing.

*Pompous prick*, she would say when he headed back to his office.

When I first started seeing him, I did not tell her. I put it off for as long as I possibly could. When he brought me flowers for my birthday, she laughed. *Oh, God, I think he's got a crush on you*, she said. I blushed and turned away from her. A week later, she saw that my address had changed in the staff files. I told her that I had moved in with him and she did not say a word.

Since then, she has stopped making faces behind his back when I am around and she has stopped calling him a pompous prick when I am within hearing distance.

But I do not kid myself that her feelings towards him have changed.

Nor have I ever tried to talk about the reason why I am with him. I wanted to, once, but the few words I began to speak just made me feel ashamed, and I stopped.

Jocelyn is always having affairs with actors who are performing at the theatre. It never lasts. When she is feeling good, she tells me it is because she gets bored, but when she is depressed, she tells me she is lonely.

*It's a co-dependency problem*, she says. *But I am working on it*.

I know that she once loved a man. *Too much*, she says.

She was living with him when I first used to sit for her. I saw his clothes over the end of the bed, his dirty plates, his records and his books, but I never saw him. He was a musician. He worked in the evenings.

One night I arrived at her house and it was all gone. Everything that had marked his presence. I knocked on the door and there was no answer. I let myself in, calling out her name as I made my way down the long, empty corridor.

She was in the kitchen. When I saw the bruises, I wanted to call an ambulance, but she stopped me. *Just stay with me,* she said, and I did.

She told me she felt like a fool. *Please don't tell*, she asked, and I promised her I wouldn't.

I made her tea, and when she didn't drink it, I poured us each a scotch. His scotch. And then another. I told her it would be all right. Over and over again.

*I kicked him out*, she said. *Do you think I was stupid?*

And she looked at me for reassurance.

*No*, I told her, *not at all*.

And I took her hand and held it tightly in my own.

*Thank you*, she said. *I just needed to hear someone say it.*

We did not refer to it again. Once I asked her how she had been feeling. She said she was fine, and she smiled for a moment. The bright smile she always has. *I was an idiot*, she said. And then she looked away.

This morning Jocelyn is anxious because she is behind in her work. She has been preparing for an exhibition and she has not done enough.

*I am tired*, she says. *I have been up all night*.

She tells me the telephones have been ringing all morning and there has been a mistake with several bookings. She says the computers have gone down and it is chaos.

She has pinned her motto of the week over the screen.

Each Monday there is a new one. This week's is shorter than most: *Do Not Accept Second Best*.

As she talks, I am trying to see past her to Martin's office. It is open and I catch sight of his arm.

He stands up and walks to his door. As he closes it, he sees me and I see him.

*I'm sorry*, I say to Jocelyn. *I will be back in a minute.*

When we are at work, Martin likes us to behave in a professional manner towards each other. He tells me that we should not bring our home into the office, nor the office into the home.

When I knock on his door, he calls out, *Enter*, and I enter, feeling like a fool.

*Problems?* he asks, and I know he is talking about work. Financial matters. He is the person we are meant to see if we need money, or if there are mistakes.

*I am responsible for the financial vision of the company*, he says when people ask him what he does. *And believe me*, he will laugh, *I often have to be very creative.*

I close the door behind me.

*What did you mean?* I ask him. 'This cannot go on.' *What did you mean?*

I want him to take me in his arms and tell me that it is all right. I want him but I do not want him. This is the problem. We keep going round and round. And as I speak, I know what I am doing. I am making myself upset. I am making myself angry. I am bringing tears to my eyes so that he will be forced to comfort me, so that he will be forced to apologise for those four words. It will not be enough, but it will be a start.

46

But he does not respond in the way I had wanted.

*Not now,* he says.

I slam the door behind me when I leave but I make sure it is not too loud. Just enough for him alone to know what I have done. Not the others.

This is the way it is.

And I do not like what I have become.

At lunchtime, Jocelyn and I go to the bistro. We sit by a window that looks over the park to the grey of the river beyond. She talks constantly, her words tumbling out as she picks at her salad, but when I catch her eye, she stops. She is still.

*What's wrong?* she asks.

Outside it is cold. It looks as though the rain will come back.

*Nothing,* I tell her. *It is just a bad day.*

I am not looking at her as I speak. I do not trust myself to be able to look her in the face and continue lying. If I started to tell her, if I started to unravel all that was tying me up, it would be endless. You pull at a thread and you find the whole garment disintegrates in your hands. This is the way it is.

She puts her hand in mine and it is warm and sure.

*It is just a bad day,* I repeat, and she lifts her palm. I know she wants me to open up to her but I do not know how.

*You have been my friend*, she says. *Let me be yours.*

I look down at the table.

*It's what friendship is about*, she says.

*I know,* I tell her.

And she offers me a cigarette, forgetting, as she always forgets, that I don't smoke. We both smile as I shake my head.

*It's me, isn't it?* she says. *I talk too much. I don't give you a chance. Always going on and on about my own problems. You must think I'm terrible.*

And then she sighs and stares down at her plate.

I want to tell her it's not her. I want to tell her not to give up on me, but as I am about to speak, she holds up a limp lettuce leaf and looks at it in disgust. *There is definitely something wrong with the new chef*, she says.

I lift the top off the pie I have been eating and we both examine the congealed meat, stirring it round with a fork.

*It's revolting*, I say.

*It looks it*, she agrees.

And she drums the table with the tips of her fingers.

*You know what?*

*What?* I ask.

*I'm going to take them back.*

And as she pushes her chair back, she gives me a wink.

*Do Not Accept Second Best*, I say.

*Do Not Accept Second Best,* she repeats, and as she turns towards the kitchen, I can hear her repeating those words. Over and over again.

# 8

You can see the jetty in my photograph.

From a distance the pylons look like matchstick legs, splayed at the thighs, a giant centipede that has risen out of the ocean and is walking, ungainly and awkward, to the silver ribbon of the horizon beyond.

The wooden planks have been bleached by the sun. Rough and worn, hammered down by heavy iron nails. The railing, too, has weathered and splintered, the white paint streaked by rust, bitter-orange seeping down the cracked posts.

They have carved their names into the wood. *Darren waz here, Sharon, Mick is a spunk, AT 4 GB 4 ever.*

She, too, has been immortalised. I know. I have seen the initials and I am sure it is her. *FS is a slut.* The words are small and insignificant, now lost in a tangled web of other names.

Black skid marks lead to the end of the jetty. I have

heard that Gary McPherson drove his car out here, skidding to a screeching halt only inches before the final drop into the ocean. The fishermen scattered in his path, throwing themselves over the railings, rods and all. This is the story.

I do not know whether it is true.

The end of this jetty is covered by a domed tin roof. It is dented and cracked; jagged sheets of tin flap in the wind. This is the place from where the toughest boys dive. Climbing up to the cheers of the others below, they bounce until they have enough spring, some diving with the grace of an athlete, others, knees to their chests, send wild eruptions of spray flying up into the faces of the onlookers.

Diving is forbidden. So is jumping, drinking, swearing and littering. The list of offences is written on a tin sign that hangs loose from the roof of the shelter. It is covered in graffiti, the words illegible beneath the scrawl of texta and paint.

This is the jetty. In my photograph it looks small. In reality, it is much larger than it appears.

By three in the afternoon, the heat is no longer bearable. I am sitting under the boards and I am wet and shivering. It is not a chill from the ocean. I am not cold. I am frightened and I do not know what to do.

I trace a pattern in the sand, circles that link in and out of each other. I write my name underneath. Elise. Over and over. I print each letter carefully, with a concentration aimed at banishing the fear, then I rub them out, replacing them with the letters of Frances's name.

This time I write in capitals and it is a spell, an incantation, to summon my sister from the jetty, the dunes, the kiosk, as far and as wide as I can cast.

*You look like you've had a bit too much sun*, a woman says as she walks past, and I am about to speak, about to ask for help, but the woman has gone.

Here the sand is damp and hard. I can see out through the crisscross of the pylons to where the water slaps and swirls and surges against the barnacles ringing the base in crusty circles. Above my head, I can hear someone running, pounding. Hollow and heavy.

This is where the older kids come at night. This is where they do it.

Frances has told me this, in the hushed voice of a rarely given confidence. When she tells me these things, she speaks with the superiority of someone who knows. I have never asked her if she, too, has been down here, pressed against the pylons with the water licking at her ankles. I have never asked her if she has lain, flat on her back, on this dark wet sand. I do not want to know.

*She's done it,* Frances has whispered, pointing in the direction of our mother's bedroom, *down there, with him.* She is talking about our father. *That's why I was born. He did it to her, under the jetty, and I was born.* She looks disgusted. *He didn't love her,* and she speaks the word 'love' with a curl of her lip. *He just wanted to stick it into her. And she let him.*

I do not want to hear. I have my face buried in my pillow, but I cannot block out her words. They slip, insidious, through any barrier I put up.

There are soft drink cans, chip buckets and cigarette packets floating in the water. Bobbing up and down on the surface. I do not like it here, but it is too hot on the beach. I can see my rock pool from where I sit and I watch it, terrified that each time I take my eyes away, she will have been and gone and I will have missed her.

*Why didn't you ask someone if they'd seen her? Or get someone to look for her?*

Because I am shy. Too shy, and it leaves me locked, frozen, wanting to move but unable. I can hear them, out on the end of the jetty, and I know I should go and look for her. If she is anywhere, it is likely that she is there. But I do not know what I would say to them. I rehearse it, over and over in my head, *Have any of you seen my sister Frances?* unable to imagine how I would ever speak those words out loud.

*Did you go? Did you go up there and look for her?*

*Yes I did,* I tell them, *I did.*

And they lean forward, wanting to know what I saw.


I never go near that jetty now.

I never really did, but now it is a place I consciously avoid. I do not know why it has become a place I have marked, but I tread warily when I am near the edge of that circle.

I am not so different to Dorothy. She has marked the one safe area, the house, and I have marked the unsafe. People think she is mad. Perhaps if they realised how much time I have to spend avoiding my zones of danger they would not be so harsh. She has been wise in making it simple. She stays where she is. Day after day.

Once Martin tried to take me out there, out along those wooden boards that lead to a vanishing point. We were walking and he turned, as all people do, to the jetty.

*You go*, I told him. *I'll wait for you here.*

He did not understand.

*It's not far*, he said, pulling me by the hand.

I was surprised at how strongly I resisted.

So was he, and because he is Martin he wanted an explanation. This is the way he is. To say no is not enough. There must be a reason and it must be articulated.

But when he pressed me to talk, I had nothing to say. I stood in front of him, the sea breeze cool in my hair and cool on my burning cheeks, and I could not give him an explanation. Not one that would make sense.

He opened his arms wide and he circled me close. He did not ask me again and I was grateful.


Sometimes I wish I could enlarge my photograph so that I could see the details more clearly. I know it is foolish but I think there may be something out there, under the outline of that tin roof, or under those boards, that I have missed.

Impossible, I know, but on some days my search back through that day is more desperate than on others.

*Yes I did go up there*, I tell them.

*Tell us*, they say, and I try.

Step by step through that day.

Over and over again.

# 9

There is a moment of perfect dark before a performance begins. A black silence. This is the time when I am uneasy. A few seconds where I wait, tense, for what will follow.

I have seen every show that has been on at this theatre. Often with Jocelyn but also by myself. I sit at the back, near the soft green light of the exit sign, and when the first lights come on I can feel myself breathe again.

I used to imagine I would be an actor. Jocelyn is the only person to whom I have admitted that. Sitting in her kitchen drinking beer, I would sometimes imitate people at work, making her laugh. When she asked me if I had ever thought of performing, I started to tell her that I had once wanted to, but I stopped myself. I remembered my mother.

*I was going to be a dancer*, Dorothy would say, over and over again. *See,* and she would lift her skirt up high, *I have the legs for it.*

Frances and I would keep our faces turned towards the television.

*Your father fell in love with these legs,* and she would light another cigarette, sighing as she exhaled a curl of yellowing smoke. *He thought I had the grace of a ballerina.*

Frances would turn the volume up another notch.

*See,* and she would kick off her sandal and point her toes. *I have a perfect arch.*

We knew what would follow.

*Now see what has become of me,* and that final sigh would fill the room, as thick and acrid as the smoke from her cigarette.

*Now see what has become of me,* Frances would mimic, mouthing the words without a sound, and I would watch her out of the corner of my eye, not daring to move as I waited for her to run her fingers through her hair, a perfect imitation of our mother behind us.

I usually leave the theatre as soon as the performance has finished. If I were with Jocelyn, she would stay. Sometimes she invites me to go and drink with her in the bistro. She sits up at the bar and talks to Nathan, one of the barmen, offering him quick drags on her cigarette when they are sure no one is looking.

They talk about their work. Nathan is a dancer as well as a barman. Or their latest love affairs. *Men,* they both say. *Can't live with them, can't live without them.*

Jocelyn is friends with most people who work at the theatre, but she is closer to Nathan than she is to the others.

I like it when it is just the two of them. It is when

other people come and join us that I find myself awkward and unsure. So, when she asks me, I usually tell her I am tired and I have to go home. She does not argue.

*But I like how shy you are,* Martin once said to me. A long time ago.

We had been at a party at Jocelyn's and I had stood in the corner for most of the night. I had watched her and her friends and I had wanted to be like them.

*But I like how shy you are*, he had said. *It's charming, old-fashioned.*

I had felt myself shrivel up with his words.

*I would rather you over her any day,* and he had squeezed my knee affectionately. *God forbid that you become loud and brash like her*, he had said, referring to Jocelyn.

I could feel his wife's gaze, staring at us from the framed photograph opposite, and I could not help but wonder whether she, too, had been charming and old-fashioned, or whether, loud and brash, she had not been able to bear it any longer and had escaped.

I once asked Jocelyn whether she had known her.

*Yes*, she told me and I could see she felt uncomfortable. *She was a costume designer.*

I had wanted to hear more. I had wanted the fact that she had loved him to make me love him.

*They weren't together for long,* Jocelyn said. *They weren't suited,* and I thought then that she must have been my opposite, the person I wanted to be, and I took comfort in that.

But this was just my imagination. To be honest, I

know very little about her, despite seeing her face, there in that photograph, every day. I look at her and she looks at me. This is the way it is, and I have never asked Martin to put that picture away. I want the fact that she has loved him to make me love him more. She is a necessary part of our home.

It is dark when I leave the theatre and I walk quickly through these wide empty streets to the number 12 bus stop. I have not told Martin that I will be late. I want him to be anxious, worried about where I am.

This city is deserted at night. I am on alert. Listening and watching, hating that I am here alone, despite having done this many times before.

The streets are wind tunnels. From the foothills to the sea, the wind whips and whorls as though it is sweeping across a flat empty plain, oblivious to the small cluster of buildings and miles of surrounding houses that mark the existence of this place.

A newspaper stand clangs loudly against the pole to which it is tied and the awning on the bus shelter rattles, lifting, threatening to fly off, and then falling down again.

I wait. The number 12 to Martin's house, where he will be reading his book in his favourite recliner chair, one bar of the heater on, just enough to warm his feet, but leaving the rest of the house cold. Across the road, the number 12 to Dorothy's, where she will be sitting under the flicker of the kitchen light, pasting her clippings into her book.

One or the other. It is always one or the other.

And I am, for a moment, tempted to turn it all upside down, to cross the road and head in the wrong direction, to where the wind throws the sea into a dark confusion and the few who dare to be out are bent low to avoid its force.

But it is just a momentary temptation. I block it out because I cannot bear to think that my escape is not my escape, that the place from which I have tried to escape is now the place to which I am tempted to flee.

The awning overhead lifts high in the wind but does not fall again. It snaps and is hurled down the street, clattering to the ground before flying off again. And as the bus pulls up, I think, *That is me, I will snap too, this cannot last, it cannot last any longer.*

But I get onto the bus and pay my fare. The dramatics are, as usual, confined to my head, the exterior continues to do what it has always done.

I sit near the front, and with my cheek resting against the window, I am resigned to heading the way I am expected to go. Home. To Martin.

Who is, I imagine, waiting for my key in the lock.

Who is, I imagine, worried that I am not home.

Who is, I imagine, in love with me again.

But when I reach my destination, it is not as I had anticipated. The house is empty. Dark, cold and silent.

I stand at the front door and let the unmistakable fact sink in. Slowly.

And I am suddenly frightened that he has done what I have always been afraid he will do. Left me. Alone.

# 10

Dorothy puts her scissors down and closes her eyes.

I doubt she is aware of the storm outside. I doubt she is aware of how high the tide is, right up, licking the edge of the dunes.

There are two piles of clippings in front of her. 'Possibilities' and 'Similar Stories'. Sorted and ready to be pasted.

If I still lived there, now would be the time when I would come in and tell her I am going to sleep. Most of the time she would let me know she had heard with just a slight nod of her head. But sometimes she would draw me in close and, unaware that I am no longer a little girl, she would press me tight and ask me for a goodnight kiss.

She could have been a dancer.

This is what she told us. I do not know whether it is true.

She keeps old photographs in a tin under her bed. I know, I have crawled under there and taken them out. Secretly. Laying them one by one across the worn carpet, trying to see her as she was. Small faded black and white prints, and I can only guess as to who is who and what is what. Her parents? Her friends? Distant relatives? I do not know. I make up stories.

She is not in many of them and in the few where she features, she is blurred. She is struggling out of her parents' hold, she is running across a neatly clipped back yard, she is swinging upside down from the highest branch of a tree, she is impossible to pin down.

*I could never keep still*, she would tell us, lamenting how much of her life was now without movement, trying to let us know that she was not what she had become, tired, beer in one hand, cigarette in the other, calloused feet resting on the coffee table. She would put her glass down and brush her hair from her eyes. I would watch the ash crumble from her cigarette to the floor and move the ashtray closer to her.

Frances would look away in disgust.

*When your father met me, he could not believe how alive I was.* Her voice would blur into the television, indistinguishable, a story we had heard over and over again, and she would rub her hands down the side of her work uniform, *The Continental Deli* embroidered on the breast pocket. *They were all trying to catch me, all the men there, but he was the only one. From the moment I saw him, I knew. He was the only one.*

She would sigh and she would remember. She would

60

see him again, unloading the truck at the back of the shop. She would be watching him, flirting with him, loudly, clearly, without restraint, oblivious to the disapproval of the other girls. She would be giggling at his jokes, hanging around where he was, hanging around, down under the jetty where the sand was cool and wet, her face flushed from drinking, flirting with all of them in the hope that he would notice.

And she would be pressed against the pylon. Alone with him, just out of sight of the others. With the weight of him crushed against her, she was unable to utter a sound.

*He loved me, your father*, and she would sigh, speaking those words again and again. He loved me, he loved me, he loved me.

There is a photograph of him by Dorothy's bed.

The few uncertain memories I have of him cannot be relied upon. They involve him as he appears in that picture, doing things that you would expect a father to do. But sometimes I cannot help but feel I have made him up, that he was something other than what I would like him to have been. I do not know.

Dorothy would butt out her cigarette.

Alone, pressed against the pylon, just out of sight of the others. Sometimes I wonder whether she knew what was happening.

You can want something but not know what it is until you have it. And then it is too late.

She would sigh and pull herself up from the armchair. Worn out from remembering, worn out from talking, she would leave us on the floor in front of the television, and wander, with no purpose, into the kitchen, where she would look, momentarily, at the dishes piled high in the sink.

*Frances, Elise,* her voice would cut through the still of the night, *come and clean up. Now.*

Frances would not move.

I would go. I did not want what was bound to follow if we did not respond. But my obedience was often not enough.

*Frances,* she would shout again.

*I'll do them*, I would say, running after her, straight into her in my eagerness to stop the fury that I knew was rising.

*For God's sake*, she would say, her hand raised, hard and sharp.

But it would not fall. It would be stilled.

She would see her, Frances, pushing me to one side, standing there in my place, her face white and angry.

I would watch as they looked at each other. I would watch and I would hope it would end there. I would hope it would not go any further. Frances pushing past us both, slamming the back door behind her, climbing back through the bedroom window hours later.

*Please*, I would say.

And my voice would be feeble in the silence.

Dorothy opens her eyes slowly. She sees how late it is, and she hears the wind. There are a pile of dirty dishes in the sink. Teacups, glasses, plates that have accumulated at a rapid rate throughout the afternoon and evening. She will leave them where they are.

She folds up what is left of the newspapers she has clipped. One by one. *The Courier-Mail, The Sun, The Herald, The Mirror, The News,* a day of news clipped bare.

She turns out the light and the house is in darkness.

In the kitchen, empty now, the tap drips.

The pile of papers has been left on the floor.

Skeletons of what they were.

# 11

Here now, in Martin's mother's kitchen, I know this is not the first time we have reached this state. It has been like this before. But each silent rift dents the whole more out of shape, until you find that you have only the pieces left in your hand.

I fear that this is where we are headed. And I know, without a doubt, that I have guided us here.

I used to move furniture when I was little. Left in the house on my own, I would push the table and the chairs to the place where I thought they should be. I would drag the lounge with a herculean strength that did not belong to a girl. I would move the armchair and the rug. I would shift and rearrange until, exhausted, I felt satisfied.

When Dorothy came home she did not notice. Details such as the position of the kitchen table were unimportant to her.

Frances would notice but she misunderstood. She

would look at me with silent approval, perhaps a quick wink and a smile, sure that it was an attempt to trick Dorothy, and I did not correct her.

I no longer move furniture when I am alone. Now I clean. I clean Martin's mother's already immaculate house with a fury verging on the crazed. I take everything out of the fridge and wipe the shelves down. I empty the pantry. Neatly stacked jars of herbs, rice, beans, caffeine-free tea and coffee.

*You have to invest time and energy in your body now,* Martin tells me. Over and over again. Despite the fact that he drinks far more than he should. *It's like opening a bank account for old age.*

I wipe each jar, one by one, and then the shelves. There is no dust. Housework is one of the few things Martin and I agree on.

Outside, the wind is furious. I can hear it, but I am trying not to listen. I am standing, sponge in hand, wondering what to clean next. I am wanting to obliterate my anxiety in a storm of Ajax and warm water.

I am not asleep when Martin comes home. I am sitting up in bed, arms clasped around my legs, waiting and listening.

He stumbles, unable to find the light switch, and hits his shin on the side table. I do not call out, *Is that you?* I stay still.

He is in the bathroom, brushing his teeth slowly, methodically. The plumbing groans, high-pitched and grating, as he turns the tap on, off, on again, off again. He does not waste water. *The driest state in the driest continent,* he tells me. Over and over again.

The door clicks shut behind him and he is padding, softly, down to the kitchen. A glass of water with a squeeze of lemon. *To flush out the system.* A gargle, and then swallow. Kitchen light off, back up the hall and to the bedroom.

*Are you awake?* he whispers.

I do not answer.

I watch as he undresses. Clothes neatly folded over the chair and then softly, softly into bed, until he is there, right next to me, his skin cold and clammy, his breath stale. He has been drinking again. I can smell it.

*Where were you?* I ask him, pretending I have been asleep and he has woken me.

He tells me he has been at a friend's. I do not doubt him. As he speaks, I shift further away from him until I find I am lying right on the edge of the bed.

*You should have told me*, I say, knowing the accusation in my voice. Knowing where I am leading us.

He says he is sorry. He tries to put his arm around me but I move further away. So far now that I have one foot on the floor. And it is cold.

*Don't*, I say, knowing what I will say before I say it because this is not the first time we have reached this state. But tonight, with the wind tossing the highest branches of the gums so they scrape against the roof, I want to take this one step further. I am pushing us to a new place.

He turns away from me. He is doing no more than what I am asking him to do.

The clock in the corner of the room clicks over. It is

12.27. I can see it, numbers illuminated by a sickly green light, and I am watching it and waiting.

He is, as I expected, asleep. 12.31 and he snores.

I kick him. Not hard. But hard enough. And he wakes.

*I can't sleep*, I tell him.

Again, he tries to put his arm around me, and for one moment I am tempted to sink. To let myself be folded up in the circle of some comfort.

I am aching for it.

But I pull away.

And my words are small and mean. I do not want to repeat them. They are small and they are mean and they are meant to hurt, the branches of the trees scratching and scraping overhead as I speak each one out loud.

*You don't love me any more*, I say.

And he rubs his eyes, tired and drunk and confused and wanting to sleep. That is all he wants, just to sleep.

But not tonight. Tonight I am dragging us further.

*Why*, I ask, *are you staying with me?*

He looks at me and I can see he does not know who I am. He has not known who I am for some time now, and the gap between what he once saw in me and what he now has is becoming impossible to traverse.

*For God's sake*, he says, and he tries to bury himself under the pillow.

I wait in the silence for what will follow.

*I don't know why I stay with you. I wish I didn't.*

And I have it. There in the dark, in the palm of my hands, I have it.

He does not love me.

He could not love me.

He has said it.

And as we look at each other in silence, I remember when we stood near the beginning of that jetty and he circled me in his arms. I had thought that it would be enough. A small circle of comfort and I had thought that it would be enough.

# 12

When I try to explain, I find I have no words.

I know I cannot give them what they want. I cannot say, *I saw this,* or, *I saw that,* just as Dorothy cannot say, *I do not leave the house for this reason,* or, *I locked myself away when that happened.*

When they ask me what I saw, I tell them I saw nothing.

When they ask me what I heard, I tell them I heard nothing.

They lean forward and they are disappointed.

*Are you sure?*

I take two steps, three steps along the jetty towards the boys at the end. Holding the rail and watching them, rehearsing my sentence, over and over in my head.

*Have any of you seen my sister Frances?*

Someone races past, running, boards pounding, everyone making way, through the group standing at the edge to the break in the barrier, and then he dives, high and clean into the water below.

*Onya, Johnno!* And they all shout, wild and loud, *Way to go,* as the older people taking leisurely strolls along the jetty shake their heads in disgust.

*There ought to be a law against it.*

I recognise him, the tallest boy, the one Frances likes, leaning against the railing drinking beer, as Johnno pulls himself up the ladder and onto the planks, lying down and feigning exhaustion after his dive.

I cannot go up there, cannot tug one of them by the T-shirt and, with a trembling voice, ask for help. Frances would never forgive me. *You what? In front of Him?* I can hear her voice and I can see her face, pinched tight with fury and shame.

*Okay, okay, okay,* he says, the tallest boy, and he puts his beer down, arms up in the air, and saunters, slowly, to where the planks end and the sea lies waiting below. He stops, poised, until he is sure they are all looking, and then, back to the sea, with a cat-like grace, he leaps high, a backflip, and then straight down.

He hauls himself up the ladder, the faintest hint of a smile on his face, and looks at them. All of them watching him. And in his look, there is a challenge. *Anyone else want to try that?*

No one does.

If Frances were here, it would be different.

She would spring high, high into the blue sky, double flip and then down with a fearless speed they all envied. I have seen her and I know that in her defiance she is

70

better than all of them. She has a fearlessness that I long for, that I admire. And that also scares me.

But she is not with them.

He draws back on his cigarette, one hand running slowly down the waist, the hip, the thigh, of some girl who looks bored and uninterested.

This is the way you have to look. I know, Frances has told me.

*You've got to make it seem like you don't care*, she says. *Never let them know*. And she is good at it. But there is a difference between real lack of interest and feigned lack of interest, and I have seen it. I have seen her indifference towards in Him, the tall boy, and I have seen it towards Will Mills, the doctor's son from down the road. Freckled Will who follows Frances everywhere, cracking smart jokes in an attempt to impress her.

But with Him there is a difference. Frances looks bored, but she is watching him. He pulls himself up out of the water and she is there, smoking a cigarette and talking to someone else; he is looking for his beer and she is standing right near it; he has had enough and she has already decided to leave, seconds before, in anticipation of his move.

He has a tattoo on his arm. A crooked anchor.

*His dad did it to him when he was drunk,* Frances has told me.

I stare at it, fascinated.

Once Frances tried to scratch a similar mark into her ankle. Razor blade, teeth clenched, and blood. I watched in awe.

71

*You tell and I'll . . .*

I promised. Crossed my heart. Hoped to die.

It did not work. It is never called a tattoo. To do so would be to admit failure. It is a scar. An accident with a piece of glass. Pissed and cut herself with a beer bottle.

But I know.

Just as I know that Frances sneaks out at night to visit Him. Just as I know that Frances would be furious if she were here now. If she could see Him with that girl. She would pretend that it meant nothing to her, that she had not even noticed, and she would turn all her attention on to someone else, anyone, even *That clown, Johnno*, rather than let Him realise.

But she is not here. And I am standing alone on the jetty, without her, not knowing where to go or what to do.

*Did you ask them, any of them, if they had seen her?*

I take one step, two steps more, towards the outer edge of the group. A shy boy, skinny and trying too hard, who hangs around, eager, waiting for his turn to jump, wanting it, but knowing it will never come. Fat Tony, belly slopping over the top of his too tight jeans, hangs with him. I know him. His family owns the fish and chip shop on Grange Road and he works there after school. If I go with Frances, he always gives us an extra piece of fish, wanting it to be noticed but not wanting it to be noticed. Sometimes Frances also manages to bludge a packet of cigarettes. Sometimes he offers without even being asked, desperate to impress, desperate to be as bad as she and the rest of them are.

I know he has seen me, but he will not acknowledge me. Not in front of all of them. I understand and I back away from him, turning around to go back down the jetty to safety.

But it is too late.

*Hey, it's Franny's little sister.*

Stopping me in my tracks.

*What yer doin' up here?*

I am scarlet, crimson to the core.

*Trying to be like her older sister,* and they all laugh.

*Steve's the one to teach her that,* and Johnno nudges Him, the tall one, snicker, snicker, and I wish I was somewhere, anywhere else but here.

*Gonna give us a jump?*

They are, I think, going to come and throw me in, and in my panic, I am trying to talk, stumbling for words to explain that I am just looking for Frances. Has anyone seen Frances?

But they are not interested in me after all.

It is Tony they have turned to. Fat Tony who is grabbed, pushed and shoved towards the edge of the jetty, and I see him squealing, great rolls of fat wobbling. *Stand back, everyone! This is gonna be a fuckin' big splash. Tidal wave, mate, bigger than the one Nostradamus predicted,* and Tony is clinging to the railing as they push, heads burrowed into his flesh, so that it is impossible for him to hang on. He's going in. I do not want to see. I turn my head and try to block out the sound of the splash.

*Who's next?* they shout, wild-eyed with the success of the last push.

And the skinny boy knows it is him. He fidgets nervously, unsure whether to run, to struggle, or simply to laugh. They seize him and he gives in, too awkward to know how to play the game, wanting it to be over, yet dreading that they will do what they always do: get him halfway there and give up, bored with his lack of fight.

*Nah — too bloody easy*, and they drop him so he loses his balance and falls on his knees.

But it is a trick.

Just as his body relaxes, they turn, one grabbing his arms, the other his feet, and with a quick wink, his jeans are yanked off, tossed to someone else, swung high in the air and then tossed again.

He kneels, trying to cover himself, and I cannot bear it. *Please . . .*

They land at my feet. One wild toss too far, and the jeans are there, on the ground at my feet. In a moment that is too quick for me to realise what I am doing, I swoop down and grab them, thrusting them into the arms of the boy before anyone can stop me.

There is silence.

All eyes are on me.

*Stopping the fun, hey?* It is Johnno who advances and he is grinning. I step back until I am up against the railing because I cannot tell, just cannot tell, what kind of grin it is.

*Leave her alone.*

I think it is the tall boy, Him, who has spoken, but I do not look up, not straight away. Better to stare at the ground, better to keep backing away, moving down

74

towards where there are people, and I want to turn and run, run as fast as I can, but I do not want them to think I am frightened.

*Hey.* And I look up at him, Johnno, standing right near me. Still grinning. *Come 'n see us when yer older.* He winks slowly. *When yer more like yer sister. We'll talk about fun then, hey?*

I do not move and I do not answer him. We stare at each other, until his grin dissolves and he backs off, with a shrug of his shoulders, and swaggers over to the group.

I also turn. I want to go home. I do not want to wait for Frances any more.


*Yes,* I tell them later when they ask me if I am certain that I saw nothing.

*Yes,* I tell them later when they ask me if I am certain that I heard nothing.

They are wanting particulars, facts, clues that might help them.

And I have none to give.

# 13

It is morning. Weak wintry morning.

The cream satin curtains that belonged to Martin's mother are drawn, but I can see the milky light of day through the gap where they meet.

The storm has gone and it is quiet.

The first morning that I woke in this room, I felt I was waking in someone's parents' bedroom and I had to be on my best behaviour.

He brought me breakfast in bed. Tea and a boiled egg on a tray, and I was careful not to spill anything, not a crumb, on his mother's pink quilted bedspread.

The night before, our first night together, he had told me he was overwhelmed.

*You are so beautiful*, he had whispered over and over again.

In the dark, his face had looked different. I had looked at him, his face above mine, and I had not known who he was.

*Martin is the kind of man who says 'I love you' on the first date,* Jocelyn once said to me.

And she was right.

But even so, even knowing the flimsiness of those words, I had held them, just for a moment, in the palm of my hand. Like a gift.

But that was then.

This morning is the morning after our fight and I am alone. Lying in Martin's mother's bed, looking at the soft light of the sky through the gap in the curtains, and not wanting to move.

I did not sleep, and when I sit up and see my face in the mirror on Martin's mother's dressing table, I am not surprised at how tired I look.

He, too, did not sleep. I know. I felt him toss and turn next to me all night. Twice we found ourselves lying face to face, eye to eye, and, not liking what we saw, we both turned away. This morning, when he woke, I too was awake, but I kept my eyes closed and my back to him.

*Aren't you going to work today?* he asked.

I did not answer him.

I can hear him in the kitchen. He is eating toast and drinking herbal tea. His morning brew. The paper is spread in front of him and he is trying to read.

I open the curtains and they slide, silently, across the window to reveal the complete expanse of grey.

This is how he finds me when he comes to say goodbye. Sitting here, on the edge of the bed looking out at the empty sky, knowing where I have led us, but unsure as to what will follow.

*I will tell them you're sick*, he says. He seems about to say something else, but then changes his mind.

I, too, am about to speak, but it is impossible to pick my words. There are so many things I could say.

We look at each other, both silent, and then he turns. Gone, out the front door and into the cold morning. I listen to his car start, I listen to him pull out on to the road, I listen until he is gone and I am alone, here in his mother's house.

And as soon as he has gone, I want to run after him and tell him I am sorry.

I sit in the kitchen and it is cold. Bare lino floors, laminated cupboards and nylon netting curtains. I hate this room. I hate all the rooms in this house. It is not my house and it is not Martin's house. It is still the house of his dead mother.

I brought almost nothing when I came here, and if I leave, I will have almost nothing to take away. The things that I own are still in a cardboard box at the back of the wardrobe in the spare room. A painting I bought with my first pay, a vase that someone gave to my mother and my mother gave to me, a few books and a large white platter.

I came here with that box and my clothes. A single car load.

Martin put my clothes in the space he had cleared in the wardrobe and he put the box in the other room.

When I took out my painting and showed him, he frowned.

*It doesn't really go, does it?* he said.

He was right. There is beige and cream striped wall-paper on most of the walls in this house.

From Dorothy's to here.

But he is not, as he likes to think, the only person I have been with. There was a time, before Martin. I have never told him. I have never told anyone. I do not like to think about it, and on the few occasions when I remember, I feel ashamed.

He was Polish and he studied Design at the Institute of Technology. He was older than I was. He was older than most of the other students there.

I had seen him but I had never talked to him. We did not know each other, but one afternoon he came and sat next to me under the clear green shade of a plane tree on the Institute lawn. He told me about himself and I listened, too shy to respond in any other way.

He told me he was going to see a play that weekend and he suggested that I come along. And I wanted to. Really wanted to. But when the night came, I could not bear the thought of turning up and seeing that he had not meant it. He would be there with other people and he would be surprised to see me, perhaps even embarrassed, and I would hang, useless, shy, awkward, on the edge.

So I stayed at home. Anxious. Distressed. All night.

I did not believe that someone like him could want someone like me. Even when he telephoned the next day to ask what had happened. Even when he drove down to Grange and we walked along the beach. Even when we ate fish and chips together in the square at Henley, drinking beer and watching the seagulls swoop and squawk in the heat of the late afternoon, and I felt I was living the life of someone else.

Even when he kissed me. Outside the Chinese Palace restaurant.

*Why are you so shy?* he asked. *It's not so scary.*

But it was. More frightening than I could ever have explained to him. I was terrified, certain that every word I spoke would be the one that would send him away.

He took me to a party the following weekend. I went against my better judgement. It was all I had dreaded it would be. A long dark corridor and a kitchen filled with people I did not know. I leant against the fridge, watching some boy pull every jar of vitamins out of the kitchen cupboard and swallow one of each, dancing wildly and shouting that he was cured, while everyone laughed and I, too, tried to laugh, until he pulled me into the dance with him, whirling me round, and I wanted to die with the weight of my own clumsiness and awkwardness.

So I went and sat outside. To hide on the back steps under the black night sky, waiting there until he eventually came and found me, drunk and miserable.

*I can't do this,* I told him, my words slurred and heavy.

He took me to his house and undressed me slowly, carefully, in the darkness of his bedroom.

*You should have come and got me*, he said.

But I could never have done that.

And he put me to bed, lying next to me, under cool white sheets. Kissing me up and down, until I told him things that made me burn with shame when I remembered, days later.

The next morning I sat, head aching, in his kitchen while he talked. He explained that he thought I was beautiful but he could not be with me. *I have a girlfriend. She is away, and I should not have done what I have done. I am so sorry*, and I knew that I had been right. It was a mistake. He did not want me. Once he had seen who I was, he did not want me.

I did not speak to him again, and I did not speak of him. Ever.

He tried, once, to talk, but how could I? He tried and I walked away.

So there has been, for all intents and purposes, just Martin. And I am sitting in his mother's kitchen, thinking about this place to which I have brought us, when he telephones.

And I think, at the first sound of his voice, that he is going to tell me it is all right.

But he tells me something else.

*It's your mother*, he says.

And I hold the edge of the table, waiting for him to continue.

# 14

Dorothy also woke early this morning.

I know this because she wakes early every morning.

Her room is dark, winter-morning dark. It is at the front of the house, on the other side of the corridor to the room in which Frances and I used to sleep. Whenever I picture this room, I see it with all the light blocked out by her heavy blue velvet curtains. They are too grand, out of place in the rest of the shabbiness, but she loves these curtains.

*I bought them when I got married*, she would tell us. *I saved for months. I told the shop I wanted them to be the colour of the lakes in northern Italy.*

But they must have made a mistake. They are the colour of mould. Cloudy. She does not see it and I have never told her.

In the darkness of her room, Dorothy lies still, eyes open, not moving. I do not know what she is thinking.

Her mind wanders, floating over all that was, both real and imagined, and this is the way she stays, sometimes for hours, sometimes only for a moment, until the sound of a car, a door slamming, a dog barking, shifts her. From then to now.

It is cold this morning. Sitting on the edge of the bed and listening to Martin leave, I shiver.

Standing at the back door, Dorothy's breath comes in frosty clouds. She bends down to pick up the papers, eight of them delivered each day. When she has finished with them, she will stack them in the sunroom. The piles cover the floor.

*My God*, Martin said when he first saw them, trying not to trip over as I rushed him out the back door.

The second time he came, he cleaned them up for her. He sweated all afternoon, pink and hot, as he carried them out the back for rubbish collection.

She ignored him.

When he finished, he flopped on the couch, a sweet, acrid odour permeating from each of his pores, and asked her for a cup of tea. Still she ignored him, knowing that I would make it for him, knowing that I would thank him for all he had done. And I looked out at the sunroom, wanting to be appreciative, but I could not think what to say. It was bare. Naked. Embarrassingly so.

Dorothy puts her coffee on the stove. I know this because this is what she does every morning. She makes it thick and black so that it coats the bottom of the cup like tar.

*Good lord*, Martin said when I once made him a cup.

*It makes my liver curl up in horror.* He threw it in the sink.

Dorothy has a cigarette with her morning coffee. There are none left in her pack, and none in the pack that she keeps hidden on top of the fridge. She has more, a stash on top of the kitchen cupboard. She thinks I do not know about them. She drags a chair over, and climbs up, on tiptoes, fingers searching in the far corner.

And this is when it happens.

The chair topples.

Like all accidents, it happens in a time of its own, one quick over-balance that is played out slowly with time enough for her to hold her entire life in her hands and think, *This is it. It has come to this*, before landing with a thud on the linoleum, cigarettes flying down with her. Packets strewn across the floor.

This is how he found her.

*It's a damn good thing he comes every day,* Martin tells me on the telephone, *otherwise who knows how long it could have been?*

John Mills, standing at the back door, paper bag of sandwiches in one hand. He knocks, as he always knocks, and waits. But there is no answer. He tries the door, but in swinging closed, it has locked. He knocks again. Nothing.

He looks up at the cool winter sky and wonders what he should do. The side window is open but he does not know whether he is agile enough to climb.

Twenty years ago, he had run up the road with me running by his side, white-faced and frightened. *It's Mum,* I had said, and he had grabbed his doctor's bag, and tried to take my hand, both of us running fast in the hot still night.

But that was then. He is now twenty years older and his leg is stiff with arthritis.

He walks nervously around the house, calling her name and testing each possible entrance. The bedroom window is the easiest, lowest to the ground and wider than the others. It is open. But still he hesitates.

*Silly*, he tells me when I call him after hanging up from Martin, *but I felt I shouldn't go in without being asked*.

He heard her before he saw her, and at the sound of her voice, relief flooded through him. She lay across the kitchen floor, her face chalky with pain, her arm bruised from where she had hit it on the table.

*I think it is a crushed vertebra*, he tells me. *Ideally, I would get her into hospital for an X-ray.*

But when he suggested it, Dorothy stared straight through him.

*Please?* He implored.

She pulled her hand away from his.

*She wouldn't go?* I ask him. I know what his response will be, but I am hoping that perhaps I am wrong.

*I didn't want to push it*, he says.

So I pack my bag and call a taxi. She will not move and I must go down there.

# 15

*It's a damn good thing he comes every day.* It is not the first time Martin has said this about John Mills and it will not be the last.

He is right. And I am grateful to him.

But.

*I don't understand why you are so uneasy with him,* Martin says.

I cannot explain.

To attempt to explain would be to reveal too much.

I would have to tell Martin about my photograph, the photograph I have of Frances and me.

I would have to tell Martin that this photograph was taken by John Mills.

I would have to tell Martin that he did not ask us if he could take it, and I did not ask him if I could have it.

John Mills likes to walk along the beach by himself, camera in hand, stopping occasionally to capture what he sees, the dried grasses swaying gold against the brilliant sky, the glitter of the sun on the ocean, a single seagull squawking angrily, a moment that he wants to hold.

I know because I have seen him. Sitting in my rock pool, I used to watch him, solitary and peaceful on a beach that was crowded with families and their activity.

The photograph I have is the only photograph he took of the two of us. There were others, but they were of Frances. I remember them clearly, even though I saw them years ago, there in a pile on his kitchen table. I looked at them all, quickly, furtively, while he found his doctor's bag, and I slipped it, the one I wanted, the one I have now, into my pocket, moments before he came and took me by the hand, leading me back up the street to Dorothy.

John Mills is good to us.

But there are those photographs.

I have never told him that I saw them, and in my silence they have become a barrier between us.

Sometimes I think that he was just intrigued by her. That he saw what I saw, the fearless defiance that drew you to her. Perhaps he simply wanted to capture that, as compelling as the glint of afternoon sun on the surface of the ocean.

But sometimes, when my search for her overwhelms me, I have doubts that I do not want to have.

Because he is good to us. He is a good person.

And I am grateful for all he does for us.


I shake out my towel. It is time for me to go home. Fine white sand flies out in the first of the afternoon sea breeze. A beach tent flaps gently, and a man with large sunglasses peers out to see if there is, perhaps, a change coming after all. But the sky is still unrelentingly clear.

I put my sandals on slowly, hoping that in these last few seconds Frances will suddenly appear. I pull my dress over my head, fearful that in the instant my eyes are covered, Frances will walk past without stopping. I roll up my towel. There is no more I can do to delay, and I turn slowly to walk back up the beach.

It is emptier now. The few families that are left are drowsy with the day's heat. Even the children are resting, curled up on towels under umbrellas, tracing pictures in the sand. In the distance, the noise on the jetty has died down. Only a few of the boys are left and they do not jump any more. They lean idly against the railing, drinking beer and occasionally jostling each other. Half-hearted and lazy.

A couple lie, nestled in each other's arms, at the edge of the dunes. They kiss, unaware of the world around them. Her legs are entwined with his, and his with hers. Further along a man sits by himself, a bottle of beer in one hand. He leans back against a cushion of sand. He does not look up as I walk past.

But I steal glances at everyone I see, hoping that one of them will be Frances. Frances smeared in coconut oil, smoking a cigarette and reading a magazine nicked from the kiosk; Frances lying flat on her stomach, brown back bared to the sun; Frances kissing one of the boys in the dunes, bored and uninterested as he runs his hand down between her shoulder blades and hopefully pulls at the tie on her bikini top.

But she is not there.

I pause before turning up the path to the road, wanting one last look before I give up. It all stretches before me. The blue sky, the sparkle of the sea and the miles of sand. And there is no sight of her.

The dry grass stings my legs and I walk with my head down now, watching each step to avoid stumbling in the gaps between the slats of wood, until I come out at the top of the path near the kiosk.

A group of kids hang out near the front, eating ice-blocks, hamburgers, chips. I know that Frances will not be there, but I wander over, just to check. This is the hang-out of the good kids, the ones who don't get into trouble – *The place where you belong*. Frances laughs at the hurt look on my face. Besides, the owner is a *Bloody perve*.

I want to know more but Frances will only expand on a good day, when she is feeling talkative, which is not often. *You know,* she says, *an iceblock for a quick grope in the back room, a packet of fags if you touch him, that kind of stuff.*

The plastic ribbons flick across my arm as I walk in the doorway, shy, just wanting to look quickly and then leave. But it is not crowded enough to hide, unnoticed in the back corner while I scan the shop, hastily, for Frances, and I accidentally catch the eye of the owner's wife.

*Can I help you?*

*Nothing,* I tell her. *I don't want anything.*

Outside a group of girls stare at me as I stand on the

footpath waiting to cross the road. They whisper and look at each other before breaking into laughter. I glare at them, but they have turned away.

I walk home quickly, along The Esplanade, down Grange Road, counting each step I take. If there is an odd number when I reach that tree, Frances will be waiting for me at home, if the number is even . . . If I count to twenty by the next corner, Frances will get home five minutes after me, and I make my steps bigger, larger, but I have only counted to eighteen by the time I reach Seaview Street.

I pass Tamara's and Mrs Brownsword is bringing the shopping in. She calls out, wanting to know where Frances is, and I point towards home because I do not want to have to stop and explain but she beckons me over and I have to pretend I have not seen so that I can just keep walking.

I want to get home now.

I need to know.

And as the gate swings shut behind me, I call out Frances's name. And again, but louder. I am not even listening for an answer, because in my heart I know there will not be one, but I think that if I keep shouting her name, it may make her appear. So I walk around the house, calling out, *Frances, Frances,* until finally I stop, once again at the back door and alone.

It is locked. Frances has the key. I push each of the windows along the sunroom but they are all firmly closed.

The bedroom window is open an inch, and I drag an

old wooden box from near the back gate around the side. I have seen Frances scramble in and out of here a hundred times, late at night, cheeks flushed, unaware that I am awake, watching her as she undresses, the sand from her jeans spilling out onto the carpet, her cigarettes carefully hidden at the back of the cupboard, and then into bed, eyes closed like she has been there the whole time.

But I have never done it myself. I push the frame up and it is stiff, swollen with the salty air. Head first, I wriggle through and tumble down onto the floor before I have time to balance myself.

*Were you worried?*

I nod my head.

*But why?*

I look up.

How can I explain?

I always knew. She was a person to whom something would happen. I can make no more sense than that, so I say nothing, nothing at all.

# 16

I ask the taxi driver to drop me at the shops.

*Here?* he says, momentarily confused because I had, initially, given him Dorothy's address.

I nod my head and he pulls over.

I know I should rush straight there, I know John Mills is waiting for me, I know I said I would not be long, but I delay. I buy flowers for her, wilted sickly pink carnations, the only bunch in the bucket outside the deli. I buy apple juice and a magazine. I do not know what she would like or want, so I keep adding items to my small pile, a block of chocolate, biscuits, lemonade, in the hope that one of them will be right.

There is a rack of postcards by the cash register and I look at them while I wait. Dusty and curled at the edges, they show summer in another place, another time. Victor Harbor ten years ago, Moana, Port Elliot, Glenelg. In all the photos the sand is white and the sea is blue, once brilliant cobalt, now faded and tinged, dirty glass green. The name of each place is written at the bottom. The script is gold and elaborate.

There are no photographs of this beach. It has never been a tourist destination. Despite its length and the calm of its gulf waters, it is and always will be a suburban beach, shabby and unremarkable.

*Is that all?*

I look up.

Mrs Thompson, who owns this shop, stares at the postcards in my hand. Her eyes are fixed on the bent corners as though I am responsible for the damage.

*Is that all?* she asks again.

*No*, I tell her and I add the cards, one by one, to my pile.

*Thank you*, and her voice is curt as always. I know her and she knows me, but she takes my money without a smile. This is the way she is.

I squint when I step outside. There is a hint of winter sunshine, a flat white glare that washes out this wide empty street, draining the road and the shops of the little colour they have. I know each of them; Doreen in the chemist, Frank in the post office and Mr Hill in the newsagency. I know them and they know me and as I stand in this street, I feel the weight of that knowledge, heavy and solid.

It is never easy coming back here, but to come back now, at this time, is particularly difficult. I do not want to leave Martin. Not now that I have pushed us to this point, the cliff edge, the brink. I am afraid that if he stands there too long without me, he may jump. You can want some-thing but not know what it is until you have it.

*Perhaps*, Martin said, when we spoke on the tele-phone, *this would be a good time for us to assess our relationship.*

My knuckles whitened around the receiver.

*I don't think either of us could honestly say that the last few months have been happy ones.*

*What do you mean?* I asked him.

*I am just saying that this may provide us both with a much needed break. A little clear headspace, Elise.*

I felt the panic, the first stirrings of what could amount to a hurricane in the silence of his mother's house. Or, as he would say, a storm in a teacup, a moun-tain out of a molehill. All inside me, but he knew.

*Now calm down*, he said.

*You are just being silly,* he said.

*I am at work*, he said.

And the taxi beeped its horn, there at the door, to bring me back here to this place.

*We will talk later,* he promised.

And I think to myself that when we do talk, I will try and take us back to where we were, away from this edge, to somewhere safer, because I do not know if I could bear to be left standing alone on this cliff. I do not know if I could bear turning around and seeing her place, the place he took me away from, the place to which I would have to return.

But it is not just my fear of leaving Martin that makes me drag my feet.

I dawdle, I delay, walking slowly up the small hill that leads to Seaview Road with my head down, but it is not just him, it is her, too. It is Dorothy. She is at one end and he is at the other, and they both pull at me. I am trapped between the two and I hover, weightless and still, like the space between the two magnets that the science teacher gave us, years ago. Caught between two poles, and the metal rod did not move. I remember. Feeling the resistance and feeling the pull. Feeling the space in between. All in that hot sticky classroom.

*Check this out,* Michael Stick had said, his voice a slimy whisper near the back of my neck. *Magnetic repulsion.*

I had turned around and wished I hadn't. He had taped a piece of paper over the south pole on each of his magnets, my name written on one, his on the other.

I remember.

*Look at this,* I had said to Frances when I got home that afternoon, my two magnets hidden in my bag.

She had wanted to magnetise the buckles on Dorothy's sandals so that her feet would stick together. It didn't work. Nothing, just a slap from Dorothy to stop us giggling as we watched her putting them on.

*What is so funny?* Her voice exasperated when she realised we could not be silenced because even separated I could still hear Frances laughing in the other room and then I, too, could not stop. Both of us, laughing until we were sick.

I remember that, too.

I look up. I have been staring at the pine needles that curl like discarded snake skins at my feet, staring at the cracks in the bitumen, staring at the weeds that push through the cracks in the rotting fences, staring at all this and seeing nothing.

I am filled with memories.

This is the way it is.

*Elise is vague*, Martin says to friends. *Head in the clouds*, and he squeezes my hand affectionately. He enjoys it when I forget, when I am slow at realising a point. He likes to be in charge of the practical.

Standing at the gate to Dorothy's house, I look down the road and I want to see it as it is now. I want my head to be clear and I want to see it as though I am seeing it for the first time.

One hand on the latch, I am perfectly still.

Salt in the air.

Flat winter-white light.

Potholes in this footpath, where the great roots of the trees have cracked and heaved their way through the cement.

A straight road that stretches north to south, with not a bend in sight.

Lavender in the next-door yard and I can smell it now.

Houses that sag and paint that peels. Salt on the windows and a lonely cactus in an otherwise bare front garden.

This is where I have come from.

It is spread before me in all its ordinariness, unworthy of even a postcard.

I open the gate slowly and I tell myself there is nothing to be frightened of.

Nothing at all.

# 17

My father came from northern Italy, from the lakes near Como. This is what Dorothy has told me.

*He used to kiss my eyes*, she would say, and she would look at us, wide-eyed so that we could see and appreciate their different hues. *One green and one blue, see?*

I would look at her as she asked, but Frances would not lift her gaze.

*This one*, and she would point to her left eye, *is the colour of the trees, and this one is the colour of the deepest lake.* She did not shift her stare. *Your father loved my eyes. They reminded him of home. That is what he told me.*

And Frances would roll her own eyes, dark-brown like my father's, in disgust.

Dorothy's eyes are closed now. She lies still in her room, her curtains, which have never looked like the Como lakes, drawn tight against the last of the day. Flat on her back, she is sleeping the heavy sleep that follows shock and pain-killers.

*She will not wake for several hours,* John Mills told me, his voice a whisper in the quiet of her room.

I looked at her. She is not old, but lying there as she was, she seemed old, and I took her hand, her wedding ring hand, and held it in my own.

From the framed photograph by her bed, my father looked at us.

There are no other photographs of him. There are no photographs of the two of them together. There is only that photograph and Dorothy's words. Her endless words.

I sat by her side and I held her hand. She turned, slightly, in her sleep, and I stroked her hair.

*She will be all right*, John Mills told me. *It is just going to take time.*

Still and quiet. I looked at her and wondered where her mind was. Another night, a long time ago, *The night that you were made*, she would whisper to Frances when she was asleep. Lovely, deep and dangerous. A night to dance along the jetty, bare feet on the boardwalk, dancing high and low under the yellow moon.

*That was the night of you*, and she would kiss Frances on the cheek, unaware that I was watching, silent and still, from the other bed.

Warm whisky and cold cold sand between her toes as he pushed her up against the pylons, away from the others. Where no one could hear.

*I am sorry*, she would whisper into Frances's hair, and

half asleep in my bed I would not know whether those were her words or whether I had only imagined them, because if they were her words, I did not understand them.

There are stories and there are truths, but the two can become so tangled it is impossible to know which is which.

*And how was I made?* I asked her once.

She did not look at me.

Three years after their wedding and he had barely been back. Quick visits in between jobs.

*We had no money*, Dorothy would say. *He could not bear to be away but we had no choice. It is a testament to our love that we survived that time*, and she would look at us both, each of us in turn, daring us to challenge her.

I am four years younger than Frances, and I can only assume that I was made on one of those infrequent visits home. And then he was gone again. Gone for such a long time that I do not remember seeing him or even knowing of him until just before I turned four, when he came back for what seemed to be a few months. A few months that were not as happy as Dorothy would like us to believe. But I do not know. My memory cannot be trusted. It is comprised of not just my scraps, my own desires for what was or should have been, but also other people's words.

My father died working on the lines. Somewhere miles from home.

*An accident*, they told Dorothy.

I do not know if I was there when they told her, or whether it is only my imagination that sees him on a crane, bright orange under the blue sky, the tip touching the wires, and his panic as he jumped down, one foot on the ground, the other on the metal body.

I do not know whether I really saw Dorothy, white and still, listening and not believing.

I do not know whether I really saw Frances, sitting at the kitchen table, drawing and singing while they told her. Drawing and singing until Dorothy told her to shut up, slapping her, the white marks of her fingers stinging her cheeks.

I do not know these things, just as I do not know what Dorothy thinks and dreams as she lies in her bed in a pethidine sleep.

In the kitchen, I put the carnations in a vase. Their crumpled edges have already started to turn brown and their heads wilt on stems too slender to support their weight.

John Mills tries to explain what has happened, but I am only half listening.

*It is really just a question of rest*, he says and I nod my head to show that I have heard.

He turns the salt and pepper shakers over in his hands and watches me as I start to put the food away. I know he is going to ask me how long I will be able to stay here for, and I am dreading the moment.

He tells me she is going to need twenty-four hour a day care for at least two weeks, and I nod again, feeling the dread tighten at the base of my throat.

*Obviously you are going to have to work*, he says, *and she won't go to hospital.*

I have emptied my plastic bag except for the four post-cards. I do not know what to do with them.

*What I would suggest,* he says, *is that I come here during the day and you look after her at night.*

I am surprised by the generosity of his offer. *Are you sure?* I ask him, apprehensively.

He insists that it is no trouble at all. He will bring his reading here, letters that he wants to write. It will make no difference to his life, he assures me.

I do not have the words to tell him how grateful I am.

*It is only for a couple of weeks,* he says, and seeing my postcards at the bottom of the bag, he picks them up.

*Is she giving these away now?* he asks, and I know he is referring to Mrs Thompson in the shop.

I tell him I bought them and I am embarrassed as I speak.

*No doubt you touched them and she used her inimitable standover tactics,* he laughs. *Curious what happens to the colours, isn't it?* He holds them up to the light. *Everything distorts with age,* and he leans closer. *Or perhaps that is just the way they were.*

He sighs as he pokes his glasses back up to the bridge of his nose and, as he pushes his chair back from the table, the lino lifting under its legs, I know he is about to leave.

*You know where I am,* he says, *if there is anything you need.*

And for a moment, I want to ask him to stay, just a little longer, but I cannot think of the words I need.

*I'll pop in over the weekend,* he promises as we stand at

the back door, looking out across my mother's pebbled yard in the last of the daylight.

He walks to the gate, his feet crunching on the ground beneath him. In this half-light, the yard looks even more desolate than it does in the day. Bare except for the rusted Hills Hoist and the scraggly pigface that winds its way through the wire fence.

The gate squeaks as he closes it behind him. He is gone, walking back up the street to his own house, where he, like Dorothy, lives alone.

I turn on the harsh light in Dorothy's kitchen and I lay my postcards on the table.

*Dear Martin*, I write on top of the first one.

I look at my handwriting, neat, round and childlike, and I find I have nothing else to say to him.

Dorothy's newspapers are piled on the edge of the table. Next to them are her two latest books, 'Similar Stories' and 'Possibilities', the clippings sorted into two piles, ready to be pasted. They are part of who my mother is. It is only when I am forced to see them through someone else's eyes that they become an oddity, *An eccentricity*, as Martin says.

I take the largest pile, 'Possibilities', and in the quiet of this house I begin to read: a movie star with a mysterious past who looks, just a little, like Frances would have looked; a woman who came from nowhere and made millions; an anonymous spokesperson for people on the streets. As the hope has diminished, the links have become more tenuous.

I read and I wonder whether Dorothy believes in any

of them. I do not know. Like many things between us, we have never discussed why she keeps these clippings. She searches in her newspapers and her letters, and I hold my photograph under the light, the photograph I stole from John Mills because it seemed to capture something of that summer and those days on the beach. It helps me hold that day, the day that it happened, right there, so that I can go back, and keep searching.

I push her pile of possibilities away from me, and I look at the clock.

There has been no sound from her room. She must still be asleep, lying in her bed, with the photograph of Franco on the dressing-table next to her.

I want to call Martin. I need to tell him I am sorry. I miss him and I want to come home.

# 18

*And there was no sign of her, nothing at all?* they ask me later, and I shake my head, eyes to the ground.

I concentrate, trying to remember every detail of the house and what I did, but they are no longer interested. I can see it when I look up.

They want to go back to the beach, and I cannot explain to them that I need to see the day as a whole. It is important to me. To go over that day from beginning to end.

They thank me and tell me that they will talk to me again soon, and I am silenced. They do not want to hear any more.

I am shown out to where Dorothy waits, wanting to tell them that I haven't finished. But I can see it would be useless. The rest must remain in my head, where I will replay it, as part of the whole day, from beginning to end. Over and over again.

In the late afternoon, the front of this house is *drenched* in sun, *bathed* in sun. They are not my words, they are words I have heard. Words used by adults in the cheap romances set on tropical islands, dog-eared and read by Dorothy late at night, and then secretly smuggled into our bedroom by Frances. Both of us in fits of giggles as Frances whispers cries of passion and clutches her stomach in the pain of love.

*I am the master of the house*, she says, *and you are the Hawaiian servant girl.*

I am dressed in a tablecloth, Frances has drawn a moustache across her lip. This is the way the roles are divided and I do not challenge them.

*We love each other*, she tells me, *but no one must know*, and we roll on the bed, gasping and sighing, until she pushes me away.

*As if*, she says and she throws the book on the floor in disgust. *It's not like that at all.*

She rubs off her moustache and I stand like a fool in my tablecloth.

The game is finished. And she leaves me. Because this is the way it ends. Always.

I am standing alone now. In our bedroom. I close the curtains because I cannot bear the brightness. My head hurts. It is 4.30 and Dorothy will not be home for at least another hour.

I had hoped for some sign that Frances had been back and then gone out. But it is all as we left it that morning. Untouched. My side of the room, neat and organised, Frances's a mess of dirty clothes and schoolbooks. My bed, smooth and tidy, Frances's a sprawl of sheets and blankets.

Once Frances drew a diagonal line, *Your side and my side*. I had the door and Frances the window. The battle was over the wardrobe. *You never even use it,* I said. *You leave everything on the floor.* But Frances wanted it. It was where she would hide things. Stuffed in the back of her side. Under a pile of T-shirts, in the toe of a sock or shoe. A new hiding spot every day. To avoid being caught.

So the line was redrawn. A diagonal with a bump at one end. I had one half of the wardrobe, she had the other. And I thought, *Right, if that's the way you want it, that's the way it will be,* so every time Frances headed for the door, I stopped her.

*My side*, I would shout, hands on hips, guarding the invisible barrier. But Frances would push straight past me. Because the line was only ever there when it suited her. Hers to cross when she wanted, and mine to respect.

I take my bathers off on Frances's side of the room. They are stiff with salt, and clumps of sand fall out in a heap. I kick them into the tangle of clothes on the floor. There is a damp patch on the carpet from my towel and I am pleased. I shake it out, vigorously, and a fine spray of sand flies across the mess of Frances's things.

Out the back it is cool. It is *drenched* in shade, *bathed* in shade. They are no longer the right words. But it does not matter. I hang my towel and bathers and watch the line swing lazily, once round, in the breeze.

It is quiet. I make a sandwich in the kitchen. White bread, and a slice of cheese. I put everything away and wipe the bench clean. There are no crumbs. Not a smear of margarine, and when I have finished eating, I wash and dry my plate. I remove all traces, knowing there may be trouble when Dorothy comes home but not knowing who it will be directed at or for what reason. It may be Frances for not doing what she was meant to do, or it may be me for not waiting as I was told. If it is directed at me, I want it to be brief and contained. Trouble for not waiting and nothing else.

With our mother, it is impossible to predict. Frances is locked in her room for stealing Dorothy's cigarettes, then she is patted on the head the next day for not going to school. *You are too much like me,* Dorothy says, wistfully one day, furiously the next. We are hugged, passionately, tightly, by Dorothy in the middle of the night, *My babies,* and then ignored, forgotten for days that pass in a vague haze of burnt pans, overflowing ashtrays and longing sighs.

So I do not rely on anything. Nothing is solid. I keep my life as self-contained as I can, a capsule that may be tossed and turned and thrown about, but that will not burst open, not leak, not break.

In the living room, I also close the curtains. The cool is soothing. I sit on the floor and try to watch the television, but I am listening for the swing of the back door, or the sound of Dorothy's car, jumping up at every noise in the hope that it is one of them coming home. And that everything will be normal again.

Dorothy's sandals lie at my feet. Strappy, high-heeled, the shoes she wears on days when she feels good. The days when she gets up and puts on bright lipstick and long black lashes. When she brushes her thick hair back and up, set in place with a mist of hair spray. Sickly sweet as she kisses us goodbye.

*I was a beauty once*, and on those days I look at her and think she is still beautiful. Glamorous. Like a movie star. Like Ginger on *Gilligan's Island*.

But on the bad days . . .

I try on one of the sandals. They are too big. But if I stretch my leg out and squint I can almost see what they could look like. And I get up slowly, unsteady on my feet, and stagger into Dorothy's room to look at myself in the full-length mirror.

Frances also has a pair of high-heeled shoes. I know. I have seen them hidden at the back of the wardrobe. Denim with lace-ups around the ankles. She has never worn them, never shown them to anyone, but they are treasured. I have seen her steal glimpses of them, and once I caught her trying them on. Walking around the bedroom in her shorts, practising, so that when she finally makes them public she will wear them without a hitch, with the same fluid walk she has in her sandshoes.

I walk up to Dorothy's mirror, trying to perfect the same stride. But it does not work. I do not have the same ease. And I am not as thin as Frances, *A little lump of lard*, and Dorothy tickles me under the chin. *You won't get into trouble*. It is a joke, an affectionate joke, but I do not like it; I squirm out of her grasp.

I sit at the dressing-table and pick up Dorothy's lipstick. Fuchsia. A dark pink on my lips, and I wipe at the corner of my mouth where I have missed, before blotting the colour with a tissue. The way Dorothy does it. My mouth is huge, alarming, and I like it.

The comb next, and I tease my hair, up and back. It is a mess of knots. But again, if I squint it could be something else. A do. And I spray it liberally, until it is lacquered stiff, unmovable.

Eye shadow. There is a choice. A silvery blue or a green. I opt for the green. Moss. It is too dark. I look bruised, and I rub at it with my finger, until most of it is off and my eyes are sore, tender. The blue is more pleasing. It shimmers, sparkles, and I turn on the light next to the dressing-table to get the full effect. *Unreal,* I whisper to myself, trying to imitate the voice that Frances uses when she is excited or impressed.

The eyelashes are the last, and again there is a choice. The mascara, or the long thick lashes that lie in the little plastic case next to Dorothy's hairbrush. They are what I would like to use, but I have seen Dorothy put them on and take them off, *Ouch,* as she peels them back, and they frighten me. The mascara is easier. Three thick coats and my face is finished.

Messy. If I look too closely. But if I step back, out of the light . . . I could be at least sixteen. And I stand and admire. Teetering in the high heels.

Dorothy's dressing-gown hangs on the back of the door. Ice-blue satin and I pull it down and wrap it around myself. There is only one more thing I need to complete the picture. A cigarette. And, unlit, I place it carefully between my larger than life fuchsia lips and

109

pretend to draw back, slowly, seductively, before letting out a delicate trail of smoke and a heartfelt sigh.

*Darling,* and I pick up the photo of Franco on the dressing-table, *you know I love you. I will always love you.*

And in the intensity of my own world, I do not know, do not hear, that the back door has slammed and Dorothy has come in, bag of shopping on the kitchen floor, and wandered absent-mindedly down the hall, looking for us, until she stands, right there at the bedroom door, and she sees.

And, not recognising me, she shouts, *Frances!*

So loud that I drop everything, the cigarette, the photo, and turn, caught, sprung, terrified, to face my mother.

# 19

When Martin asked me to move in with him, he did not know what he was asking. He had met Dorothy but he did not know what it would mean for me to leave her. Even now, I do not think he knows. Not really.

He first mentioned it when he took me home after our weekend in the country.

We had spent the morning walking to a deserted slate-mining village. He and I and Marissa and Robert, walking high into the rolling hills behind their house. Hills the colour of wheat, gold under the sharp blue sky.

Martin talked, his voice loud and clear in the stillness of that village, each word ringing out, echoing against the crumbling bluestone walls of what had once been houses. I do not remember what he was saying. I tried not to listen.

*This was the church.* Marissa led me away from the others and I stood with her, shielded for a moment from

Martin's words, and looked out through the window to the soft sweep of the hills tumbling down, one after the other, into the shimmering ocean beyond.

*From this distance the grass looks like velvet. Soft enough to lie in.*

She looked at me, surprised I had spoken, and smiled.

*Listen.* She turned away, staring back out the window, and I listened.

It was not loud, barely perceptible, a slight moan, as the wind weaved its way across the smooth flow of the grasses and through the empty walls. There was nothing else, just its sigh in the stillness, and I did not want to move; I wanted it to fill me. I leant against the wall, cool despite the heat of the day, and I closed my eyes.

But the peace did not last.

*There you are*, Martin said, his face still pink from the exertion of the walk. *Praying for forgiveness, or more money for the arts?* He chuckled, amused by his own wit, and took my hand, his palm sticky and hot around mine.

I did not answer him.

We left that afternoon, straight after lunch, Martin wanting to beat the traffic.

*You must come again*, Marissa said to us.

*Any time*, Robert added.

And Martin promised them we would. I sat silent in the car, knowing they were lying and wanting to apologise, but not knowing what it was I wanted to apologise for.

Driving home in the heat of the early afternoon, I closed my eyes and pretended I was asleep. I did not want to see the cars and trucks, the petrol stations and the used-car yards. I did not want to hear Martin. I did not want him to say to me, *See, it wasn't so bad, nothing to be scared of at all.*

I did not open my eyes until we came back into the city, waiting at the traffic lights where the road that leads to Dorothy's house stretched in one direction and to Martin's mother's house in the other direction.

*Sleepy?* he asked and patted the top of my leg.

I nodded.

I had expected him to take me home, but when he turned the car towards his own house, I stopped him.

*I can't*, I said. *I have to go back.*

He did not understand, and I did not know how to explain that she had been there, alone, all weekend. It had been, in fact, the first weekend I had ever left her.

*Perhaps*, he said when we pulled up at Dorothy's gate, *we should talk about you coming to live with me.*

He had been kissing me, his mouth hot and suffocating on mine, his eyes closed. I had felt the seat belt cutting into my shoulder as he pulled me towards him and I had tried to undo it but had not been able to find the catch.

He opened his eyes when he spoke and I did not want to meet his gaze. I was embarrassed by his desire. I tried to open the door to let some air in. With the airconditioning off it was hot and I felt I was going to faint.

*What do you think?* he asked, leaning forward to kiss me again.

*I have to go,* I told him, pulling away, knowing I could

113

not find the words to explain how difficult it was for me to answer him.

He let me go but he did not give up. Once the question had been asked, there was, for him, no going back. Every time we saw each other, he mentioned it.

It is not that he wore me down. It would be unfair to say that. He would take me home, and sitting in Dorothy's kitchen, watching her read and paste, I would dream of my escape, but I could not find the moment and I could not find the words.

*Have you told her?* he would ask.

I would shake my head and promise that soon, very soon, I would speak.

But it took me six months. Six months from when I first promised Martin to when I actually told Dorothy that I wanted to move.

I do not know how I found the courage. I suppose these things build up. I had imagined my words a thousand times, so many times that eventually they moved from the imagined to the spoken, coming out before I knew that they were no longer just words in my head.

I do not like to remember what I said. I know I did not stop. I felt that if I kept on speaking, I could make it better.

Dorothy put her scissors and paste down and walked out of the room.

*Please.* I followed her, standing right behind her, not knowing how I was going to keep saying what still needed to be said. And each of my words fell like stones, heavy and stupid at my feet.

I was met by silence. She did not speak, she did not move, she did not even blink.

*Please*, I finally said. *I know you disapprove, but please.*

She looked at me. *I have not said a thing*, she said, hands in the air, walking backwards out of the room. *I have not said a thing.*

And she did not say a thing, not another word from that moment, until I put the last of all I owned in Martin's car. It was only then, when we both stood awkwardly in the kitchen, that Dorothy finally spoke.

*Goodbye,* she said.

I told her I would visit. I promised I would be back. She did not look at me and I did not know what else to say.

Martin beeped his horn and I knew I had to go.

*I'll take good care of her*, he shouted from his open window. *You just call us if you need anything, anything at all*, and he waved. *Bye, Dorothy*, toot toot of the horn for good measure as he pulled out on to the road.

She did not wave back, did not lift a finger, and was gone, back inside the house, before I had even turned around to face the road ahead.

# 20

I do not speak to Martin until Sunday morning.

Each time I have called him, there has been no answer. On Sunday I call early and after ten rings he picks up the telephone.

We are polite. We have very little to say to each other.

I tell him I need some things, some clothes I forgot to bring, and he tells me he will bring them to work tomorrow.

I tell him I need them this evening.

We both know I am lying, but eventually he promises to drop them in.

I hang up and I hear Dorothy shift in her bed. I know she has heard every word of our conversation and I am strangely ashamed. I am about to knock on the door, but I change my mind; I want to put off the moment of facing her.

Standing on the back steps, her papers under my arm,

I look out across her yard to the next-door neighbours'. Where we have pebbles, they have a small lawn, with neatly weeded flowerbeds. Scarlet pansies against the grey sky, and I stare at them, eventually seeing that they have been planted to spell 'Bless This House' in crimson.

They are new neighbours. I remember when they moved in six months ago. I saw their little boy. A packing box squashed almost flat, rocking furiously back and forth, back and forth, on their lawn. I was watching it, unable to comprehend how it was moving so frantically on its own, when he emerged, head first, corduroy legs second. Seeing me, he ran back into the house, embarrassed at being caught in a world of his own making.

In the kitchen I try to make Dorothy's breakfast. My head is elsewhere. I find I am staring out the window at the fence and the toast has burnt.

*What are you thinking?* Martin used to ask me and I could never answer him.

He no longer asks me that question. Most nights we eat our dinner in silence. Not a word, until I cannot bear it any longer.

*What are you thinking?* I will ask him, hearing my voice rise.

*Nothing*, he will usually say, *nothing at all*, and he will open the newspaper and try to read.

I will wait, tense, for him to turn the page. I will listen to him chewing. Sometimes he will hum softly, tunelessly. My fingers will grip tightly around my knife and fork. I will push my chair back and take my plate to the sink, scraping the scraps into the bin, metal on china, scratching, dropping the cutlery into the sink so that it will clatter, slamming a cupboard door shut, turning the taps on, water spraying fast and furious; but he will not move. He will not even flinch.

But I am not there with him. I am here with her.

I remember that I have been boiling an egg. I remember that I have been making coffee. I turn the percolator off seconds before it boils over. I fish the egg out of the water. It has cracked, letting out a trail of white that has solidified into a grey mass on the outside of the shell.

I knock nervously on Dorothy's door. It swings open at my touch, and I tiptoe in, unsure whether she has gone back to sleep.

She is awake. In the dark I can just see her, flat on her back, eyes open, staring at the ceiling. She does not move and she does not speak. I put the tray on the table next to her bed and move to open her curtains, to let in some daylight.

*Don't*, she says, the abruptness of her voice startling me. *I want to see them*. She reaches out and turns on her bedside light. It burns, harsh, in one small pool, leaving the rest of the room in darkness.

*I am in pain*, she mutters, and I can see that she is. As I try to ease her into a sitting position, I am mentally counting the number of pain-killers she has had. I cannot remember. Even if I could, it would not be much help. I have forgotten how many she is allowed.

Dorothy pushes me away. *I'll do it*, she says, drawing herself up so that she can eat.

Her coffee is lukewarm now. She drinks two sips and

hands it back to me. I break off a piece of toast and dip it into the egg before passing it to her. She is irritated.

*I can feed myself,* she tells me.

With the plate balanced on her lap, she eats slowly. I do not know whether I should stay with her or leave.

*Don't,* she says, when I finally turn to the door. She motions for me to take her plate and sit next to her, patting the edge of her bed with her hand.

*I wish that I could brush my hair,* she tells me wistfully, running her fingers through the strands that have escaped from where it is twisted at the back of her neck. It takes me a few moments before I realise she is, in fact, asking me to do it for her.

*Gently,* she tells me as I pick up the brush from her dressing-table. It is clogged with fine dry hair, twisting through each of the bristles.

I untie the knot at the base of her scalp, my fingers touching her. I can see the liver spots on her once clear skin, and in the white brightness of her bedside light, there is no possibility of hiding each pore, each soft sag, each red vein.

Her hair is long and heavy in my hands, dry beneath my fingers, a dead weight.

And I am, for a moment, overwhelmed by an awareness of her mortality.

*Your father used to love my hair,* she tells me. *He used to brush it for me. He told me it was the colour of the sunset over the lakes in northern Italy.*

She is not expecting a response and I do not give her one.

*I was the envy of all the girls. I would catch them looking at it, admiring its colour, their own hair dull in comparison.*

She motions for me to brush higher, near her crown.

Her roots are grey. I have known that she is grey for some time. I buy her hair colour every month. She writes the brand and the colour on her list that she leaves for me on the kitchen table. One of the items that she does not want anyone to know about. I had, however, never realised how grey she has become.

*Once I was even asked to be in a commercial. For shampoo*, and she sighs. *Just the ends*, she instructs me.

I lift her hair up, holding the length near the bottom, and brush the ends until there is not a knot left.

*Shall I tie it back for you?* I ask her.

She shakes her head and thanks me.

As I turn to the door, she stops me one more time. One hand on the knob, I turn to face her, thinking she wants to tell me something.

But she just points at her plate on the floor.

I pick it up as I am told.

# 21

There was no moment when it happened. That is what is difficult.

Sometimes when I find myself going over that day, I realise I could never stop. I could keep going, the next day and the one following and the days that stretched before that day.

I am searching for a defined event, and that is not how it was.

I imagine other losses. A lover dies in your arms and you brush his hair back from his face, feeling the last breath, all the life, there and then gone. Your child is killed in an accident and you see the body, tiny body, laid out in front of you and you know that it has come to this. A friend leaves the country, there with you and then gone, last grasp of the hand, last kiss on the cheek, last moments before you are physically pulled apart by the reality of the departure.

I imagine these losses, and it seems that in each of them there is a dividing line between what was and what is. But that is not how it was for us.

I see Frances walking down the path to the beach. Tall and thin under a harsh blue sky. I see the bleached wooden slats of the path she walks. I see me watching her, hoping she will look back, but she doesn't. She walks towards the white sand and beyond that the glittering sea.

This is the last time I saw my sister.

It is a moment. But it is not the moment. It is not the dividing line I am looking for. Because there was more. If she died, I want to know how she died. If she left us, I want to know when and why.

Twenty years later, I stand at the top of the path and, still, I see her.

I take my shoes off and the sand is cold beneath my feet.

Following the path she took, I walk towards the beach. The jetty and the kiosk, closed for winter, are to my left. That is the way she went, but I do not walk towards them. I turn, as always, to the right.

It is still early and there is a Sunday-morning calm. The houses on the beachfront look deserted. The curtains are drawn and the doors are closed. Most people would still be asleep. The sky is blank and empty, pearly grey over a dark grey sea. Grey on grey, broken only by a single ship that moves from left to right. The seaweed has washed up onto the beach. It stretches, forward and behind, as far as I can see in both directions. Black and knotted on the white sand, a great uneven stripe.

I am relieved to be out of the house. I have not left it since I arrived on Friday and being there, alone with Dorothy, weighs heavy on me.

*I will be back soon*, I promised, wondering why I worried about leaving her alone. She is used to it, after all.

I walk to where the sand and the grass are no longer divided by road. The Esplanade has stopped, returned to nature by the council. The grass grows thick and coarse, unruly and unmowed up to the neat clipped lawns of homes that are wealthier here, new and obvious in their attempt to blend into the surrounds. Designed by architects, painted pale-blue or grey, with great windows and decks that are usually empty, they are the kind of houses that Martin likes.

A young woman in pale-pink tights and a sky-blue T-shirt stretches and limbers up. Headphones on, she jogs up and down a few times before setting off along the beach. She is chased by a dog that barks furiously, running in and out of her path. A little boy wheels his red tricycle around and around the cement at his front door. From far off, a man calls out, *Jesus, that bloody dog*, and his voice rings out, loud and clear, in the stillness.

I walk close to where the sea curls up on to the shore and then slips back out again. Slick and silent, slippery with weeds. It slides over my toes, white foam washing over my white feet. In my hand I have a stick and I am tracing a pattern, a curling line to mark where I have been. It follows me, broken in patches by the tide washing the sand smooth again.

Because I am not looking where I am going (Martin tells

me that I always have my *head in the clouds*), I do not see him. I do not even hear him when he calls out to me, and I am startled when he stops me, hand on my shoulder.

*Elise*, he repeats, and I look up at him, John Mills with his camera, framed against the washed-out sky.

He apologises for surprising me and tells me he has been meaning to come over.

We are awkward with each other, out here away from the house and Dorothy.

*I have been taking pictures*, he says. *My Sunday-morning ritual. Far more satisfying than church*, and he smiles.

We stand silent together and look out across the ocean.

He tells me he has been working on his mosaic. He has been meaning to visit but he lost track of time.

I am surprised it is still unfinished.

*Sometimes I think it is because I don't want to finish it, and at other times I think it is because I want it to be perfect. I want each colour to match my vision, and my vision grows more and more impossible.* He looks down for a moment. *Shall we walk back together?* he asks, and I nod my head.

He sees the pattern I have traced in the sand.

*So you can find your way home?* he asks. *Although it would be impossible to get lost on this beach*, and then, realising what he has said, he looks away, embarrassed.

I want to tell him it is all right, I am not upset, but before I can speak, he apologises.

*I am sorry*, he says. *It was thoughtless.*

I tell him it is okay, and I mean it.

We are silent again.

My feet sink into the wet sand, each print swallowed up seconds after I leave it. I drop my stick and it floats out with the next swell, tossed back in again moments later.

John Mills looks across to the line of seaweed on our left. *I have been photographing it*, he says. *There are some extraordinary plants. Both fascinating and repulsive.*

We walk closer to where it stretches oily and dark for what appears to be miles.

I have never liked seaweed. I remember the smell from when I was young. After the winter storms. You could smell it as soon as you got off the bus, thick and sulphurous. Once Frances collected a bucketload and left it under Dorothy's window as revenge for a punishment. When Dorothy found it, she brought it straight into the house and dumped it on Frances's bed.

*But what about me?* I complained. *Now I have to smell it too.*

Absorbed in their own war, they had both ignored me.

*What do you do with yourself?* John Mills asks me. *After work, in your spare time?*

I tell him I see plays, the ones at the theatre. It is all that I can think of. I do not know what I do with the rest of my time. Alone in that house with Martin, time just seems to pass.

He asks me what I have seen lately, and I tell him, finding that I am running through the list of names on our winter season program. I have seen them all.

*Any favourites?* he asks.

I am never confident discussing what I have liked and why. Sitting at dinner parties with Martin and his friends, I am usually silent while they talk loudly about actors, directors and writers they love and hate. Martin joins in, despite the fact he has not seen anything. His opinions are dressed-up versions of the little I have told him.

Walking along the sand, I describe the last play I saw. My words are halting and uncertain, but he listens, stopping me with the occasional question, so that I talk until we come to the path where we will part ways.

We are standing opposite The Mansions. They are a row of bluestone terraces, three storeys high. Tall and grand, they break the flat miles of beach and bungalows.

*They look as though they have been transplanted from another place,* I say.

*Do you know the story?* he asks, and I shake my head.

He tells me they were built for sea captains. *I have visions of their wives sitting on those balconies, watching for their husbands' ships to come in.*

A place to wait.

He turns to the path and then stops. *Will is coming for dinner*, he says. *If you are not doing anything, I'm sure he would love to see you again.*

I thank him but tell him I am busy. *Besides*, I say, without thinking, *Frances was always the one he liked.*

Above us, the sun is breaking through the clouds. We are squinting in its pale, clear light as we stand, awkward with each other once again.

*Do you think about her often?* he asks.

I look straight past him and lie. *Not any more*, I say.

*I do.* He stares at the ground. *I wish I could have done more.* He speaks softly, so softly that I almost do not hear him.

I wait for him to say something else, but he is silent.

Later, lying in the bedroom that was once my bedroom, and before that, the bedroom I shared with Frances, I think about his words and I do not know what he meant.

In the darkness, I get up and cross the dividing line to her side of the room.

Her bed is still there and I pull the cover back, revealing the mattress.

This was where she lay.

And as I put my head on her pillow, I remember.

Hearing her come in through the window. Watching her get into bed. Tiptoeing across in the still of the night and lifting the sheet. The warmth of the small space that she made for me, the softness of her breath in my hair, the weight of her arm across my waist.

It was all right. She was home.

And I would curl my body into hers and close my eyes.

But that was then.

With my knees to my chest and my eyes open, there is only the chill of the bed. And as I lie there remembering, I wish she would come back.

I wish she was with me now.

# 22

*Did she often come home late?* they ask us later. *Was there any reason for you to be alarmed?*

Sometimes it is just Dorothy they ask, sometimes me, sometimes both of us together.

I try to explain. I try to tell them about my sister, but I feel that I am betraying her. *She didn't do what she was supposed to do*, I begin to say. And then I stop myself.

They wait for me to continue.

I do not want to say these things. I do not want to tell them that she often broke the rules.

*It was different*, I try to tell them. *Something was wrong*, I try to say. But I am not sure if we knew that then, or whether it was only later that we could say that we knew.

The glass is cracked. Diagonally. From corner to corner. And from beneath it, my father's face looks up at us. He is twenty-three. Young and handsome. Staring straight at the camera. Staring straight at me looking down at the smashed glass in horror. Staring straight at Dorothy who does not look at the photograph, but at my mouth and eyes, lurid with colour, realising that she has made a mistake. It is not Frances standing there wrapped in her dressing-gown, but despite now knowing that she was wrong, she is still flushed with what she thought she had seen.

*Where is she?* she asks.

I shake my head and tell her that I don't know.

*Has she gone out?*

I shake my head again.

She pulls me to her, ripping the dressing-gown off, rubbing at the lipstick, the eyeshadow, the lashes with a tissue. Smearing them, scrubbing them until I am red raw, shaking me. Hair next, and she brushes with a vigour that rips at my scalp, through the knots.

*I told her to stay with you. Just one simple thing I ask her to do. But not even that. She won't even do that. And it is not so much to ask. Not much at all.* Rip, rip through my hair so that it flies out in great waves of static.

I am standing perfectly still. Not crying. Because it would take an idiot not to realise that there is trouble now, and it may fly in any direction.

*And you*, she slaps me hard on the back of the leg, *you must never, ever do this again. Do you hear me? Never.* She shakes me again, then pulls me close, tight, so that I can smell her perfume and the sour sweetness of a distress that I know. I am wrapped in her arms, not able to move and not able to breathe, until she pushes me away again and looks around the room at the mess of make-up on the dressing-table, the gown crumpled on the floor and next to that the photograph, smashed.

*I'll clean it up.* My voice is small and scared, wanting to appease, but before I have even finished speaking she is out in the hall, and I hear her, checking the bedroom, bathroom, lounge, kitchen, sunroom, calling Frances's name, over and over.

*She's not here.* I am running after her as I speak.

She does not listen. She is at the back door, then out across the yard, to the gate, where she shouts again, *Frances!* louder this time, oblivious to the sly peeks of curious neighbours from behind curtains and screen doors.

I can only watch until she turns, defeated by the silence that meets each of her calls, to where I am waiting for her on the steps.

Silhouetted in the purple dusk, she walks towards me. Her high heels slip on the pebbles so that she seems to sway drunkenly as she makes her way to where I sit, arms clutched around my knees.

She lights a cigarette and the match sizzles. She lets it fall, charred black, next to her feet. Dainty feet with blood-red toenails. *(I could have been a dancer, you know.)* In her sandals, her arch is accentuated. I am staring at it. She has her head in her hands and sees nothing. Her cigarette is burning, unsmoked, between her fingers, trails of ash falling to the steps, until it is down to the butt. She stubs it out on the cement.

There is a sprinkler in the next-door garden. It is ticking as it circles. Every few seconds, a sparkling spray of water splashes over our fence and onto the line where my towel is hung. I watch it, hoping Dorothy will not notice. I have seen her fury over this before.

*Did she bring you home from the beach?*

I shake my head.

*Did you wait for her as you were told?* There is anger mounting in Dorothy's voice again, and I find that I am inching away, until I am pressed against the peeling paint on the iron railing. A large flake drops onto my thigh.

*Did you?*

I nod. Not wanting to cry. Not now.

*Did she take you down there in the first place?*

*Yes*, I tell her, relieved that that at least had happened as it was supposed to.

*What time?*

*Just after you left.* My head is down and my words are mumbled.

*And you haven't seen her since?*

I shake my head, not trusting my voice.

*So where is she? Did you look for her? Ask her friends? See anything at all?* She does not wait for my answer. She pulls herself up and heads back into the house. I follow her, racing to keep up, into our bedroom.

She is kicking through all of Frances's things, looking for something, anything, some trouble other than this. She turns, wide-eyed, to face me. She is gripping the bottom of her work uniform with her fingers, screwing it up into a tiny ball, staring at me but not seeing me.

*Please*, I tell her, *she's just gone somewhere.*

In the kitchen, she lights another cigarette. She sits at the table and I watch, anxious that the burning end is going to light her hair. But it doesn't. Each time it gets close, she takes another long inhalation, the tip glowing bright and the ash crumbling to the floor.

We do not talk. Not a word, until Dorothy stubs out the butt. She takes her hands away from her face and looks up. Her mascara has run, black-rimmed eyes and faded cracked lipstick, and behind her the kitchen clock clicks into place, 6.45, the numbers bright in the darkness.

*I'm going to go and look for her,* Dorothy says. *On the beach.*

I want to go with her but she tells me I have to stay, to be here in case Frances comes home. She does not look at me as she talks, but rummages, distracted, through her bag, to find her car keys.

They are on the table. I push them towards her.

She takes them without glancing up, out the front door, and it slams shut, echoing down the hall to the kitchen, where I sit alone and watch the clock. 6.55.

Outside it is night now. It has crept in unnoticed, across the rows of rooftops, to where the day slips, red and splendid, into the ocean. The lights on the jetty flicker once, twice, before turning on and streaking the sea silver, the only markers for miles.

The sea laps. Quiet. Broken by a splash of a night-time swim, the rustle of the long grass and the squeak of sand underfoot. Cool, dark and soft.

Another day has ended.

I am waiting in the kitchen, swinging my legs, backwards and forwards, backwards and forwards, too short to reach the floor. I am drawing a picture of myself on the corner of the newspaper, and I am trying to convince myself that it is okay.

This is what Frances does. She comes home late.

There is nothing to be worried about.

# 23

Martin is a punctual man.

If he says he will meet me at six, he is there at six. This is the way he is.

I am also punctual. *Elise is like me*, he tells people, *never a minute late.*

It is not an attribute of which I am proud. I once told Jocelyn that I try to be late, but it seems to be an impossibility. I delay until the last possible moment, but when that last moment comes, I panic, I rush and I am on time. I cannot help myself.

Jocelyn laughed. She did not understand. She is always late. We go to a play together and she arrives seconds before it starts, out of breath and apologising. I have been waiting, agitated, anxious that she will not make it. She always does. It is just that the car broke down, she lost her keys, she lost track of time; she has an endless array of reasons.

Martin told me he would be here at five.

I am waiting for him in the kitchen. I do not want to look at the clock again. I know he is late but I do not want to know how late.

The first night Martin took me out for dinner, he arranged to meet me at seven. I was at the restaurant five minutes early. He arrived seconds later.

I was nervous. I could not imagine what we would find to discuss. I remember crumpling my serviette in my hands. I remember reading the menu three times and seeing nothing, nothing at all. I remember wishing the evening would be over so I could go home.

Martin talked. I cannot recall a word he said, but I remember listening. And when I realised that that was all I would have to do, I was relieved.

Later, when I was at home, I panicked. I lay awake, worrying I had bored him. I wished I'd had stories to tell, comments to make, anything other than my silence.

But Martin did not seem to mind. Three days later, he asked me out again.

And I remember thinking that perhaps this could work, perhaps it was enough. He could talk and I could listen, both of us fulfilling the other's need, neither of us demanding anything the other could not give.

I light Dorothy's heater and smell the sweetness of the gas for a few seconds before the pilot catches. It is cold in here. Damp and cold, and I can feel the evening chill creep under the sunroom door.

I tell myself I will not call him for another half hour.

But I pick up the telephone and as I am about to dial

the number there is a knock on the back door.

He stands with my bag in one hand and a bunch of flowers in the other.

*For Dorothy*, he says, in case there is any confusion.

I ask him in and he hesitates. It is only for a moment but it is long enough for me to notice.

He sees the pile of papers on the floor and shakes his head. I wait for him to speak. I wait for the words I have come to expect: *She really should get someone to clean these out for her. On a regular basis. It's ridiculous and probably dangerous. If a fire started, the whole place would go up in flames. Pronto,* followed by a click of the fingers to emphasise the point.

But he is silent.

He puts my bag on the floor and walks straight down the hall. *Dorothy*, he says as he approaches her door, his voice loud in the quiet. At least he has not called her Dot, or Dotty.

*How are you?* Her door is open and he walks straight in.

She does not answer.

I tell him she is probably asleep, knowing full well this is not the case. She is pretending. Eyes closed, not wanting to register Martin's presence, at all. For a moment he looks at her, lying there in the darkness of her room, and then tells me he should get going, his voice a whisper now.

*Please*, I say and I nod my head in the direction of the kitchen.

I believe I know Martin well. You cannot be with

someone for as long as we have been together without having some knowledge of who they are. I usually know what he will say and what he will do. I know his gestures, I know the cough he has when he wants to get attention, I know the way he cleans his glasses when he is hot, I know the way he twists his father's ring on his little finger when he is nervous, I know the coarse black hair that has started growing on his shoulders, I know the way he worries about this but does not want anyone to know, I know the way he fusses about his tie being straight when he gets ready for work in the morning, I know the stories he tells when he wants to impress. I know all of this and more. But lately I do not think we know each other at all.

He is agitated. And it scares me.

He sits at the kitchen table and plays with Dorothy's scissors, turning them over and over in his hands. He shifts the papers to one side of the table. He does not look at me.

Martin is a man who believes everything can be articulated. When I find I have no words, he does not understand. But now he does not know what to say and I am the one doing the talking. I tell him I have missed him. My words sound false, but I know they are true. When he was not here, I did miss him. I start putting his flowers in a vase and I keep talking. More than I usually talk. I do not know what I am saying. I am trying to pull apart the silence, puncture holes in it, until it is no more.

He puts the scissors down and looks up at me.

I do not know that look.

He tells me he is going away. *There is a conference,* he says. *Next week. I am leaving tomorrow.*

The flower stems are sticky between my fingers. There are too many for the vase. I do not know what to do with the rest. They lie on the kitchen bench, great clumps of colour, so bright that it hurts to look at them. I am surprised he chose them. Martin buys jonquils and tuberoses, pale flowers. He buys them for me and the smell fills his mother's house. Overpowering in its sweetness.

*I will be away for a week*, he says.

I do not know why he is telling me this. He picks the scissors up again and then puts them down. He stacks the clippings neatly, straightening the edges of each pile. He rests the paste on top of one and the scissors on top of the other.

It is in order. It is then that he can tell me.

And in the silence of my mother's house, he speaks the words I have been expecting but had not expected.

*I think you should move out*, he says. *While I am away.*

I am throwing the carnations I bought for Dorothy into the bin. Clearing another vase for the rest of his flowers. The water is putrid. I toss it down the sink and start picking at the rotten stems that have stuck to the inside of the china. They are glued to the side.

*Do you understand?*

It is still outside and from the kitchen window I can see that the sky is clear. If I sat on the beach now, I would be able to see all the stars. Thousands of them smattered across the black night sky.

*Can you say something?*

I fill the vase with fresh water and leave it on the windowsill. I open the window wide and let the night air in. Cool and fresh. From behind me, I can hear him pushing his chair out. I know it will lift the lino, tearing the hole even wider.

It was Frances who first made that hole. I remember. Pushing her chair back with her hands on the table, pushing it back and ducking underneath, out of reach of Dorothy who was leaning forward to slap her. I cannot remember exactly what she had done. There was always something.

My fingers are numb. Numb from the winter cold.

*For God's sake*, he says. *If we can't even talk about this, what is the point?*

I close the window as he opens the back door behind him.

I turn around and he has one foot on the steps. One foot out the door.

*Wait*, I say but I do not know whether I have spoken out loud. *Wait*, I say again, but it is too late.

He cannot hear me. Not the faintness of my voice above the sound of the pebbles beneath his feet. Not the feebleness of one word above the squeak of the gate as it swings shut.

I am whispering to myself. Over and over.

*Wait*, I am telling him. *Wait*.

But it is too late. He has gone.

# 24

Dorothy does not cry.

I believe she is proud of the fact she never cries, but when I say this, I am only guessing. It is not a matter we have discussed. I just know I have never seen tears in her eyes, not even when she learnt that Franco, my father, had died.

We were eating dinner when they came to tell us. At least, that is what I think we were doing, but I do not know whether I can actually remember the events or whether my knowledge is not, in fact, knowledge, but only a half-truth.

There were two of them. Two men who had worked with my father on the lines. They may have been his friends, or simply foremen on the job. It was Frances who showed them in, and they stood awkwardly, too large for our kitchen, shifting from foot to foot, until, in their clumsiness, they just talked. Straight to the point. In front of all three of us.

I pity them now. It is not a job I would be capable of doing.

As they spoke, I stared at my plate and Dorothy stared out the window. Neither of us uttered a sound. It was Frances who broke the silence with her singing. Softly at first, a whisper under her breath that slowly built as a breeze builds until there was no denying its existence, the same tune, over and over again.

I believe she would have kept on singing, singing until her voice reached a shout, if Dorothy had not slapped her. I can remember how she sounded. I can remember how loud she was.

But the song was broken by the sting of Dorothy's palm. The sting on her cheek that made me lift my head, and upon doing so, I saw the tears.

My sister was crying and it was something I had never seen her do before.

The men who worked with my father told us they had to leave. Their voices were loud in the silence that followed Dorothy's slap. They told us they had a train to catch and they headed towards the door. I do not blame them. I, too, would have left as quickly as possible.

Dorothy did not move. She stayed as she was, staring out the kitchen window.

Frances pushed her chair back. I did not dare look at her. I just waited until I heard the bedroom door shut, and then I followed her.

She was sitting on the floor, her arms wrapped around her knees. I could not see her face, but I knew.

When she finally looked up, her eyes were still red.

*It's my fault*, she said, and I did not know what she meant.

*I did it*, she said, and her words made no sense.

*I did it because I wanted it. I wanted him dead.*

I did not understand and she did not explain.

She was the only one of us who cried on that day.

In fact, sometimes I wonder whether those tears are the only tears that have ever been shed in that house. At least since we had been living there. It seems impossible, but it may be so.

You see, I am like Dorothy. I do not cry.

I do not know how.


It is Monday morning and I am on the number 12 again. Travelling in the old direction. From the sea to the city along the road I know so well.

Last night I sat in the stillness of Dorothy's kitchen and I laid the four postcards I bought from Mrs Thompson on the table in front of me.

*Dear Martin*. The words were already written on the back of the first one.

I picked up my pen and wrote on the second. *Don't.*

The third lay blank before me.

Half of the flowers that Martin had brought for Dorothy were still on the bench, the empty vase on the windowsill.

The first time Martin bought me flowers was the first time anyone bought me flowers. Pink roses.

*Leave me.*

I put them in my bedroom and hoped that Dorothy

142

would not see them. I do not know whether she did. She never mentioned them, but that does not mean she did not see them.

On the fourth postcard I wrote one word: *Here.*

All four cards laid out in front of me.

*Dear Martin, Don't Leave me Here.*

*Dear Martin, Don't Leave me Here.*

This morning, I put the postcards in my bag.

Rather than going to my usual stop, I walked down to the beachfront, to the terminus on The Esplanade. The bus was waiting. The engine turned off, the driver reading the newspaper in silence. He did not look up when I paid him my fare.

Sitting by the window, I looked out at the kiosk, the roller doors pulled down and firmly locked, and, beyond that, the deserted jetty. In the still of the morning it was clear the worst of winter had passed. Soon it would be summer again.

*Dear Martin, Don't Leave me Here.*

I am hoping he has not left yet, that he will be at work and I will be able to talk to him, to tell him it is a mistake. I am thinking about what I will say to him. I am planning my words, staring out the window, dry-eyed and certain that I can convince him to change his mind. That we can go back to the way we were.

But when I arrive at work, it is clear that he has gone.

*He left at seven,* Maria, his secretary, tells me.

I did not really need to ask. The door to his office is open, and I can see his desk. Everything has been put away. This is what Martin does before he goes on a trip. He puts everything in order.

I ask her if she has his number and she looks surprised.

*He gave it to me, but I lost it*, I tell her.

My voice is louder than it should be and in the open plan of this office, I know everyone can hear.

In the box office, Jocelyn asks me how Dorothy is.

I tell her.

She asks me where Martin has gone.

I tell her that as well.

*Bad time to go away*, she says, and I nod my head in agreement.

She looks at me and she looks concerned. She is tapping the desk with her fingernails. They are dirty, bitten down to the quick.

*Am I your friend?* she asks me.

*Yes*, I tell her.

*Then you should talk to me*, she says.

I look at her and I remember bathing her face when she cried in her kitchen that night. I don't think she has ever told anyone, not even Nathan, about what happened.

I look at her weekly motto, taped on the side of the computer. *I am a creative person, worthy of giving and receiving love.* I smile.

*We have had that one before*, I say.

She just looks at me.

*I am sorry*, I say. *I am having a bad time with Martin.*

*I know*, she says.

I am expecting her to give me the number of her therapist, to suggest some self-help books or even that I come

to group workshop with her. She doesn't. She is remark-
ably quiet.

And I tell her that I think we are breaking up.

I tell her that I think he wants to leave me.

*And I am finding it hard to cope,* I say. *I am finding it
hard to keep it together.*

*Tell me,* she says.

And I try.

# 25

I am sitting at home drawing myself as a mermaid. My fingers are flecked with different texta colours, a confetti of hues from my pack. A line of green has found its way to the corner of my mouth and a circle of violet near the tip of my nose. But I am not aware of this. I am the mermaid in my picture.

When they questioned us, there were always certain eyeteeth that had to be extracted. The important points. The relevant facts. This was where they wanted to pick it up again. They wanted to listen.

But not to me.

I am at home, drawing. This is not important. It is Dorothy they turn to. *Please*, they say. They nod in encouragement, and she lights another cigarette.

*From when I left the house?* she asks.

*From when you left the house.*

She draws back and exhales slowly. They push the ashtray closer to her.

*Okay*, she says, *I will try*.

I am sitting on the floor. They have given me a book, pencils, a toy to play with, but I am not interested. I am listening to her.

She is not telling a story. She is trying to tell the facts. And it is something I have never seen her do before.

I cannot imagine what she felt. I cannot know what she thought. I can only imagine how it would have been for me if I were her. This is the way it is with her and me.

Sometimes she tells them what was going through her mind, using different words every time. *Anxious, worried, frightened*. I look at her as she speaks and I try to see her as she describes herself. But nothing fits. I am not used to her saying how she really was. I am used to her telling us how she would like to have been.

She tells them and I listen, seeing her as I imagine her to have been.

I see her park the car at the kiosk and I see her sitting with the engine idling, looking out to sea. Smooth and still. There is no wind and in the quiet she can hear everything. Someone laughs and it dances out clear across the ocean. She can see the shadow of the fishermen under the lights at the end of the jetty and she watches as one casts off. The plummet of the sinker down to the depths. She wonders whether she actually heard it or just imagined it.

She turns the engine off and notices that her knuckles are white. White from gripping the steering wheel, and she shakes each of her hands and breathes deeply. *It will be all right.*

The beginning of the path is lit, but the rest is in darkness and she stumbles in the sand that piles high between the wooden slats. The heel of her sandal gets caught, and she takes them off. The bare boards are rough and the grass slaps her calves. She knows this path. Escaping down here in the hope of meeting him, running out of breath to the jetty. She remembers and it does not seem so long ago.

On the beach the sand is soft and cool and she can smell the salt and seaweed. She walks quickly, blind in the dark, and before her the ocean swells in its enormity, black sea, black sky merge in an infinity. It is like this at night. Vast emptiness and she remembers, back against the pylon, his head buried in her neck, the force of his weight, but then stops herself. That is not what she is meant to be talking about. Not that, not then. They do not want to know about that night. They are concerned with another night. Another day. Another time.

She butts out her cigarette and continues.

She tells them that she did not know whether to call out Frances's name. I know how it would have felt, futile in the darkness around her, but she tries once, and her voice is clear and strange. Disembodied. There is no answer.

Under the jetty, the water laps over her toes. There is no one there. She calls out once and hears nothing but the sea. The slow lazy slap. In and then out again. She feels helpless as she looks around her, searching for something that she knows she will not find.

On the jetty there is no one but the fishermen fishing for sharks, and as she nears them, she sees one of them reel in a catch, slippery tail flicking under the light, slip slapping as the man takes the hook out of its mouth before tossing it into the bucket at his feet. As she asks them, each of them, any of them, whether they have seen her – *Frances, she is only twelve* – she sees the fish out of the corner of her eye, jerking spasmodically in the shallow pool of water, and she does not want to watch but she cannot help herself. It is gasping for air, gills flapping, and she wishes they would put some more water in, or kill it, a quick blow on the head, rather than this.

*Haven't seen her*, one man says, and a few others shake their heads.

*Been no one here but us*, says another, and he casts his line out again, far out, singing as it flies through the inkblack, and then down, plop, into the sea below.

*Are you sure?*

He turns to look at her, no doubt seeing her not as she sees herself, but seeing her hair, thick and wild about her face, seeing the black smudges around her eyes, seeing the bare feet, and he shakes his head again before turning his back on her.

Because she looks like some crazy woman. Some crazy woman who does not warrant more than a cursory shake of the head, and realising it is useless, she turns back towards the beach and walks down the jetty alone.

They listen, waiting for her to continue.

*That was it*, she tells them, lighting another cigarette. *You didn't look on the beach?* they ask. *Just one more time?*

149

She shakes her head. *I went home.*

They wait for her to expand, to tell them more.

*I went home,* she says again. *I went home,* and she is confused by the hardness in their eyes, the accusation in their words.

I am at home and I am waiting for her. I do not want to be reminded that this is what I am doing, so I keep my back to the clock and I concentrate on my drawing.

But this is not all I am doing.

As the clock ticks over towards eight, my thoughts drift, fragile tendrils reaching out and curling around images, faint at first because I do not dare to let them crystallise, and then more solid, more real.

They are disjointed images of how life would be without Frances. Frances's bed moved out, Frances's mess cleared up, and I am opening the wardrobe to see just my clothes, my things, spread out, space between each of the hangers, shoes in a neat row at the bottom.

*You are my only one,* Dorothy says.

*What shall we do today?* Dorothy asks. *Just you and me,* and she pulls me close. *I don't know what I would do without you,* she says and I am held tight in her arms, the only one left to hear her words, over and over again.

My mother drives home alone.

I can hear the car pull up in the street.

I can hear the door slam shut behind her.

I look up from my drawing.

She is back.

Dorothy alone in the doorway, sandals in one hand, and a trail of sand behind her.

*So that is all,* they repeat. It is not really a question. It is more like a statement.

I can tell how difficult it has been for her to speak in the way she has spoken.

She nods her head but she knows it is not all. I know that and she knows that.

It is all wrong. I want to tell them that it is all wrong. You can't do what they are doing. You can't just take bits. You have to take everything. All of it. Dorothy, Franco, Frances and me. Everyone we know and everyone they know. Every day of our lives and every day of their lives.

There is no end to it.

It goes on and on and on.

But how can I begin to explain this to them?

# 26

While I am at work, Dorothy is at home.

While I talk to Jocelyn, Dorothy talks to John Mills. He is to her what Jocelyn is to me, the closest either of us have to a friend.

*I did not have girlfriends*, Dorothy would say, and she would curl her lip at that word. *They were jealous*, she would say, *petty, and I was not interested.*

At the deli where my mother worked, Mrs Hansen, once Jillie Green, would select slices of ham for a lunch she was having on the weekend, or cream cheese for a cheesecake she was making, perhaps olives, it did not matter; she would order in a loud and confident voice, and we would listen while we waited for our mother to finish for the day.

*It's eight people*, she would say to the woman behind the counter. *Are you sure that will be enough?*

We had heard my mother say hello to her, and we had

seen her nod in response. Brief, embarrassed, so quick it may never have happened.

*I think that's the lot*, Mrs Hansen would say and she would count out her money from a gold Glomesh purse, her pink fingernails clicking on the hard surface as she placed each coin in a pile.

Our mother would hang up her apron and we would follow her round to the front of the shop. Mrs Hansen would nod again, but Dorothy would pretend she had not seen.

*I was never interested in any of them*, Dorothy would say as we walked, quickly, through the shopping mall.

Frances would look at me and roll her eyes.

*They disapproved, but it was simply envy. They wished they could do what I was doing*, and Dorothy would pull at the hem of her dress, so high it barely covered the tops of her thighs.

Three steps behind, Frances would follow. An imaginary handbag over her shoulder, she, too, would pull at the hem of her dress and toss her hair. She, too, would tell me, silently mouthing the words, of the envy of the other girls.

*Don't*, I would say.

But there was no stopping her.

Later, in the quiet of our room, Frances would whisper to me, *They didn't like her.*

I would not want to hear what was bound to follow but I could not stop her.

*They thought she was a slut*, and I would block my ears. *She probably did it with all of them. Not just him,* and I knew she was referring to Franco, *but all of them. Down there, under the jetty. One by one. One after the other,* and I would bury my head in the pillow, anything to stop the sound of her voice. But it was not possible.

*No wonder they all look at her in the way they do, no wonder they all think they're better than her,* and I would see my sister's face, hard and sharp against the light of the moon through the window. Pinched and tight. Her words like the slick on the sea after a storm.

Mrs Hansen, Mrs Rowley, Mrs Donovan. Jillie Green, Sally Wildey, Carol Jenkins.

*How is your poor mother?*

They are not her friends. They never have been and they never will be.

Apart from John Mills, there has never really been anyone. Brief friendships with neighbours that burnt out as quickly as they began.

*This is Mrs Jacobs,* Dorothy would say to us, her voice proud as she introduced her new friend. We would smile politely and escape to the television, but even with the volume turned up high, we could still hear her. Dorothy talking endlessly about her marriage, her dreams of dancing, her beauty. We would listen and we would know.

*Thank you,* Mrs Jacobs would say, trying to break into the first pause, no matter how slim, in an attempt to extricate herself. *I must get going.*

Occasionally they would be back, maybe once, twice at the most, caught by Dorothy on the street and unable to escape, but usually that first visit was the last.

My mother did not have friends.

In fact, I think John Mills may have been the first person to visit her on a regular basis.

*He is a godsend,* Martin tells me.

I can always hear the reprimand in his words. Faint. But there. Because Martin does not understand why I do not appear as grateful as I should. He believes John Mills is doing Dorothy and me a good service and we should not forget it. This is the way he sees the situation.

While I am at work talking to Jocelyn, John Mills is at home with my mother.

Normally they would sit in the kitchen. Years ago, on hot days, he could sometimes persuade Dorothy to eat on the front verandah, but as this became more difficult, he stopped trying.

*There is no point,* he told me once, *in pushing her.* But I am not sure whether he actually believes that, or whether he simply knows he is not the person to force her.

Today, if he sits with her, he will have to sit in her bedroom. A chair pulled up beside her bed, with only the bedside light on to break the darkness. Or perhaps he has convinced her to open her curtains, letting in the cool blue of this late-winter day.

I do not know.

If she is quiet, he will talk to her. I know, I have heard him. He will tell her how the storms have passed and the high tides have slowly receded.

*There is a beach again,* he will say, and she will close her eyes and remember what it looked like.

*The sea is calm and there were kids on the jetty this morning. Not swimming, but it shouldn't be long.*

She will tell him that she loved to swim. She will tell him that she was the only girl who could swim from one jetty to the next.

It may be true or it may not. It does not matter. He will listen anyway.

*It helps me too,* he said to me once.

I did not understand.

*I like to have places to go each day.*

He saw that I did not know what he meant. *I have Will and I have friends, but I need to have places to go where I may be of some use. More so than I ever was as a doctor.*

He is, I believe, a friend to my mother.

Just as he is to the others he visits on his daily rounds.

I try to understand this strange sense of duty that brings him to our house. Sometimes I can. And I do know how much he means to Dorothy. But I can never imagine that there could also be a friendship in it for him. I have never been able to imagine anyone calling my mother a friend. Just as I find it difficult to see myself talking and confiding in the way that friends do.

But I try. I try to tell Jocelyn about Martin. I stumble for words and it is not easy.

# 27

When I return to Dorothy's after work, I feel that I am going the wrong way.

I am not used to travelling in this direction, not at this hour, and when I see the sea in front of me, I am disoriented. I want to turn and head back to the place where I would normally be. The place where I feel I should be.

But I am here, on this side of the road, standing at the postbox with my four postcards in my hand.

I have addressed each of them, *Martin Hislop, 14 Ferntree Road, Stonifell,* and put a stamp in the top right-hand corner. The question is whether I will post them.

They are balanced at the entrance to the chute (post by 6 p.m., delivery next business day), but each time I think I have made up my mind to let them go, I find I am still holding on to them.

*What I love about Elise,* Martin used to say, drunk and

157

proud, *is her calm. She would never do anything irrational,* and he would squeeze my shoulder affectionately.

He was comparing me to his wife, who was, by all accounts, far from calm. But Martin stopped making those comparisons years ago. It was not a temper he discovered in me. It was something else, and it was clear that it was not expected. Nor was it welcome.

With my fingers gripping the corners tightly, I put the cards back in my bag.

*It will,* I tell myself, *be all right when he comes back,* and I turn my back on the postbox and look down to the end of Grange Road, the sea still faintly visible in the fast encroaching night.

This is not where I normally stop, but coming home on the number 12, I did not want to go to our local shopping centre. There are times when I do not feel I can cope with seeing their faces, any of them, and I pulled the cord early.

I am a stranger here and I walk with my head down, staring at the scuffs on my shoes. I would not have even seen him if it were not for that instant when I look up, startled by the noise of a truck braking suddenly.

Fat Tony's fish and chip shop.

And he is there.

Out the front, leaning against the doorway, watching the slow crawl of cars down Grange Road. Above his head, the row of light bulbs along the awning flicker intermittently.

Fat Tony. Squealing as the other boys push and pull him to the end of the jetty until finally they have him where they want him and, with one last shove, he topples, over the edge and into the ocean below.

This was not the last time I saw him but it is how I remember him.

I am walking past, eyes averted, in the hope he will not recognise me, but as he flicks his cigarette into the gutter and turns to go back inside, he calls out, losing certainty that it is who he thinks it is as soon as he says my name.

*It's me. Tony,* and he grins in the foolish way he has always grinned.

I could pretend I had not heard. Or that he has the wrong person. But I don't.

I stop and smile shyly back at him.

*How ya been?* As he speaks, a little girl with black ringlets and dark eyes tugs at his hand. He picks her up. *This is Sophia*, and he cuddles her proudly as she hides her face in his neck, embarrassed at the attention. *She's only three*, and Sophia giggles as he tickles her.

I ask him if he is running the shop now and he tells me he is. Sophia is squirming in his arms and he puts her down. *Me and my wife. You remember Vicky?*

I don't but I tell him that I do.

We stand, awkward with each other, unsure of what to say next.

*So, what ya doin' round here?* he asks.

I am about to tell him I am staying with my mother when Sophia comes back, holding a crumpled Chiko Roll wrapper out towards me.

*Is that a present for the lady?* Tony kneels down next

to her, his great belly straining against his stained white apron. Sophia nods.

*Thank you,* and I take the wrapper, but she does not remove her hand.

*She's taken a liking to you,* Tony laughs.

I also laugh.

We both laugh a little too long.

*So, you doin' okay?* he asks me, and I tell him that I am.

*Fine,* I say. *Just fine.*

From the back of the shop, someone calls out his name. He looks in anxiously. I also look. All I can see is the television high on the ledge on the back wall.

*That's Vicky,* he says. *I'd better go. Wanna come in and say hi?*

I shake my head and tell him I have to go too.

*Well, see you round,* and he takes Sophia's hand and heads back into the shop.

But just as I am about to keep walking, he changes his mind. He calls out and I turn. He is nervous and wishes he had left things as they were.

*They didn't do nothin',* he says. *They were pricks but they didn't do nothin'.*

It takes a few seconds before I realise what he is talking about.

*I just wanted to tell you,* and he shrugs, awkward, aware of what he has opened up, and wishing he had not spoken.

I do not know what to say.

*I just wanted to tell you,* he says again, and he turns, feeling like a fool, to the door, just as I am thanking him, my voice a whisper in the traffic. Too soft to hear.

Fat Tony. The only one of the boys who had acknowledged what had happened. He had sent a card. Gold, with a picture of a rose on the front. *In sympathy for your loss*, written in gilt inside, with his name scrawled underneath. *Tony.*

*Who's that?* Dorothy had asked.

I had told her he was a friend of Frances's.

She had screwed up the card and thrown it in the bin. It was only four days after it had happened. Too soon for such messages. Not then. Not yet.

But I had retrieved it. Smoothed it out and hidden it in the back of the wardrobe, in one of Frances's old hiding spots.

*They didn't do nothin'.* The boys on the jetty. *They didn't do nothin'.*

I know what he was trying to say but I am so used to silence, his words do not comfort me as he had hoped. They only distress me.

And I walk home, anxious, wishing he had not said anything, wishing he had just left me alone.

# 28

We do not talk about the past.

We do not refer directly to it. Not in the way Tony did.

This is not to say it is never mentioned, it is (or at least aspects of it are), but it is only Dorothy who speaks and she speaks of a past she has created. There are great tracts we never traverse, names we never utter and events to which we never refer; some facts, some fantasies, a pile of each on either side of me. And each year the space between us shifts. It is a desert and the sandstorms are constant, changing the shape of all I know before my eyes.

I remember but I do not know what I remember any more. It becomes harder, not easier, to know what is truth and what is a lie.

Fat Tony pushed off the end of the jetty.

Fat Tony flicking his cigarette into the oncoming traffic on Grange Road.

*In sympathy for your loss*, and Dorothy throws the card into the bin. She does not want to speak of certain things. She does not want realities.

*They didn't do nothin'*, and I do not want direct words either, walking down the road towards my mother's house, hoping they will have faded into the heavy evening sky by the time the back gate swings shut behind me.

Home from work and I am staring at my face in the bathroom mirror. Under the yellow of the bare light bulb, I can see my eyes, my nose, my mouth, my hair, my skin, and I am, as I often am, overwhelmed by the sensation of looking at the face of someone I do not know.

One green eye, one blue.

My eyes are blue-green. Neither one nor the other.

I stare at myself and I cannot see the whole.

There is mould on the mirror and on the walls. The paint peels in grey strips from the ceiling. The bathroom window is cracked, diagonally, a jagged line from top to bottom, and the shower rose is tied on with a piece of string. I look at each and every one of these realities and then look at myself once more before opening the door.

John Mills is waiting to say goodbye.

He is in the lounge room, and as I walk in, I know he has been looking at the photograph of Frances, the one on top of the television, the one that appeared in the newspaper. I know because I heard him put it back. I know because I can see the clear shape of where the frame once rested, dark in the surrounding dust. I know because you cannot help but look at it, and I know because I saw him turn around, startled when I came into the room. I know we are both expecting not to speak of it, but I do not know if this is the way it should be.

*It's fine*, I say, nodding at the photo, trying to acknowledge what has happened.

He apologises, feeling he has been caught in the act of prying.

We are silent with each other and then he tells me he has to go.

Tonight it is still. I have often sat in the quiet of this house, knowing the wind is blowing great sheets of sand on to the streets and the pine trees are creaking overhead, straining against the force of the storms, while the ocean chops furiously against the pylons beneath the jetty. I have sat in this quiet, listening to the sound of Dorothy's scissors and the crumple of the newspaper beneath her hands, knowing the fury just outside our door. I have also sat here, knowing the calm outside, while inside Dorothy shouts and screams, or whirls around; words, words and more words.

But tonight there is a balance. Still inside and out.

I stand on the back steps and watch John Mills walk across the yard, the pebbles beneath his feet the only sound in the quiet.

*I'll see you tomorrow*. He waves, the gesture barely discernible in the dark, and then turns to walk down the road to his own house.

In the kitchen, I take my photograph and put it on the table in front of me.

The white border is grubby. The print is smeared with

fingerprints. It has been bent in places and the cracks cut into the image, breaking the colours.

I have looked at it so often that I no longer know what I am looking at.

Two young girls.

Frances and me, the sand, the sea and the jetty.

If you look closely, it is possible to see a flurry of seagulls at our feet. A white blur of wings against the faded pink-gold of the sand. Or maybe it is the grasses in the foreground. I do not know.

Frances and me, the sand, the sea, the jetty and the gulls.

Frances and me, the sand, the sea, the jetty and the grass.

I move the image so that it is directly under the light and peer at it more closely. Everything becomes a blur. Blue, yellow, pink, orange and white. It could be anything. I move the image away until gradually, one by one, the components take shape. The greater my distance the more I see.

But if I close my eyes, it is not the photograph I see. It is the end of the jetty and she is there. She has her back to me, and in front of her the sky and the ocean glitter, more brilliant than they are in my photograph, sparkling clear and bright. She is balanced on the railing, her feet curled around the peeling paint, her arms still by her side. She does not move.

I, too, do not move. I am holding my breath and waiting.

*Watch me.* She turns around and looks at me. Just once.

From the other end of the house, I can hear Dorothy calling me, wanting me to come to her now. I do not move. With my eyes closed, I am watching her.

Completely still, and then she springs. From the balls of her feet, up high into the sky above, a perfect arc into the sea below. There and then gone.

And I miss her.

*Elise.*

Dorothy calls me and I open my eyes.

# 29

I remember. Seeing Dorothy standing in the doorway, sandals in one hand, a trail of sand behind her. And no Frances. Not daring to ask, not daring to say a word.

I had been kneeling on my chair and I had dropped my legs to the floor, slowly standing up, all the time looking at Dorothy, who did not speak. She just stood there.

I told her to sit down, but she did not move, so I took her hand and led her to the table. I pulled the chair out for her and moved her towards it. I remember seeing her fingers curled around the top of the seat, I remember her nail polish chipped and bleeding around the edges of her nails. I remember her smell.

Distress is sour.

She took the pins out of her hair, one by one, and laid them on the table in front of her. I remember seeing the knots in her hair, gold and red twisting in and out of each other, and wanting to get the brush and to brush it out for her because sometimes she would let me do that. As a treat.

But not that night. I knew that without needing to ask.

I told her I would make dinner, but she did not answer me.

She searched for a cigarette. The pack was empty and she screwed it up. There was another in the drawer and she took one out, hastily lighting it in a flash of sulphur.

All the food was in the shopping bag on the floor. Dumped where she left it when she came home. The small parcel of chops had bloodied the butcher's paper, staining it crimson brown. I unwrapped them.

Three.

I did not know what to do with the third but I did not dare ask.

I remember putting the water on to boil the peas, my arms shaking with the weight of the saucepan as I carried it to the stove. I remember setting the table, three plates, three knives, three forks and three glasses of cordial, with her watching me, silent and still.

In my memory the kitchen clock ticked, but that was not how it was. It is an electric clock and the minutes moved forward in silence, while Dorothy smoked, stubbing out butts in a saucer, or letting them burn out, the heavy headache of smoke filling the room.

*Don't,* Dorothy said as I put Frances's plate in the oven. *Let it get cold.*

I obeyed, and that third meal sat there, directly opposite, as I tried to eat, the chop fat slowly congealing and the peas swimming in a puddle of cold water while Dorothy smoked, cigarette after cigarette, eyes fixed on the clock.

9.07 and the numbers flickered, electric dots of red. I pushed my plate away and also looked at them, waiting until Dorothy spoke.

*I am going to the police*, she said.

She threw the butts in the bin and dumped the saucer in the sink before turning to look straight at me. *I am going to the police.*

I ran to put my shoes on, quickly, not wanting to be left behind this time, wanting to be there and ready when Dorothy got in the car. Because I knew the only way I would get to go would be if I was not noticed, if I was no trouble.

This is the way it is with Dorothy and me.

This is the way it has always been.


I remember.

I can hear Dorothy call me and I leave my photograph on the kitchen table and go to her.

The light from the corridor spills into her room, dim but some relief from the darkness, just enough for me to be able to see her lying on her bed, head turned towards me.

*What is it?* I ask her.

I presume she is hungry but she will not tell me that. She does not like to go straight to the point.

*I am making dinner*, I say, not wanting to wait for her to speak.

*No, I am not hungry*, and Dorothy points to the pile of papers on the floor. *I am so behind*, she tells me.

I do not want to do this, but I find I am bending down obediently, reaching for the top one, the Brisbane *Courier-Mail*.

*Not all the stories,* Dorothy instructs me. *Just the headlines, and perhaps the first paragraph. If it sounds possible or similar*. She lies back, eyes closed, waiting for me to begin.

I move the paper closer to the bedside light, but it is still difficult to see and I am forced to bend low, eyes close to the small print, my back twisted and uncomfortable in the small space next to my mother.

Dorothy waits.

The gas heater hisses.

A moth flutters, its wings beating against the burning electric globe. I brush it away, the back of my hand accidentally knocking the framed photograph of Franco, and it teeters perilously, unbalanced for one instant as I lurch across to right it at the same moment as Dorothy reaches out too, both wanting to stop it but only knocking each other. And the photograph clatters, hard, against the bedside table.

It is Dorothy who picks it up.

I do not want to know.

She turns it over. One sheet of glass. I breathe again and Dorothy slowly, carefully, puts it back where it belongs.

We do not say a word.

Again, I stare at the newspaper in front of me. Again, Dorothy waits.

The headlines. The first paragraph. A light-plane crash in the state's north. I read the sentences, but I cannot say them out loud, and I look at Dorothy for help, but she has turned her head away, and, eyes closed, she waits.

*I'm sorry,* and in the silence, my voice is small. I fold the paper, the pages dry and unmanageable in my hands, refusing to be put away neatly.

Dorothy watches.

*I can't,* I say and I point to the papers on the floor.

Dorothy's eyes, one green, one blue, hard and still, watching, as she tries to reach out with one arm to the floor where the papers lie. Whatever pain there is, and there must be pain, is not expressed, but kept in, glittering and sharp, until she collapses back on the pillow, exhausted but triumphant, the paper in one hand.

I do not move to help her. I watch, unable to do anything else.

*Please,* I finally say, *can't we talk?*

But Dorothy has turned her gaze to the floor. *Pass me my scissors.* She does not look up.

I can see them, too far for her to reach, but I do not move towards them. *No,* I tell her, surprised at the words I am speaking. *Not until you talk to me,* and as I speak I am overwhelmed by the feeling that my voice is the voice of someone else.

She looks at me. My mother. I am reaching for her hand.

She pulls away, and the recoil startles me.

*Please*, I say again, but it is useless.

She will not look at me now.

I watch as she shakes the newspaper out in front of her and tries to ease herself up on the pillow so she can read. I watch as she runs her finger along each line, mouthing the words to herself. I watch and I feel foolish.

*I'll get dinner*, I tell her.

She does not even blink an eyelid.

And in the pit of my stomach, I know what I am in for and I know it will last.

It is silence, and it has begun.

# 30

*You should stand up for yourself,* Jocelyn once said to me.

We were at work and Martin had questioned the number of staff I had rostered on over the weekend. I cannot remember the details. It was a long time ago. It was before Jocelyn knew about Martin and me. It was when she still used to call him a pompous prick to my face.

He put the figures on the desk in front of me and circled the total in red before telling me that the wages had been too high.

*You're going to have to do something about this*, he said.

When I tried to explain that I had had approval, he would not listen.

*We all have our budgets, Elise, and as managers it is our job to keep within them. I'm afraid I'll have to bring this up at the next financial meeting.*

It was Jocelyn who interrupted him, her voice louder than mine had been when I had tried, and it was Jocelyn

who told him he should take a minute to hear what I had
to say.

*Pompous prick*, she said when he walked off without
apologising.

When I told her that I did not mind, she became
angry.

*You should mind*, she said with a vehemence that startled me. *You shouldn't let people walk over you.*

I knew she was right, but I did not know any other
way.

Staying with Marissa and Robert in the country, I felt
ashamed of how quiet I was. I would listen to Martin
speak for me and I would want to stop him but I would
not know how.

I remember eating lunch when we came back from the
slate-mining village. Sitting under the shade of an apri-
cot tree and throwing the eggplant Marissa had made
under my chair in the hope the dog would eat it.

When she had asked me if I liked aubergine, the purple skin glistening with oil, I had been about to refuse,
but Martin had spoken for me.

*We love it*, he said, and as I watched him scoop mouth-
fuls up with his bread, the oil shining on his chin, I did
not know how I was going to finish mine. Most of it
ended up on the ground and that was where it stayed.
The dog was not interested. I saw this as soon as I pulled
out my chair.

The others saw it too.

*You should have told me you didn't like it,* Marissa said.
*I wouldn't have been offended.*

I felt like a fool, my face blushing scarlet under the harsh midday sun.

This is the way it is with Martin and me. I am asked a question and he answers for me. I start to speak and he speaks for me.

*You should assert yourself,* Jocelyn says to me. And not only on that occasion with Martin, but at other times, whenever I am hesitant, whenever I fail to stand up for myself. *I know*, she says, *I learnt the hard way*.

And often, after telling me this, she will bring in her *Face the Fear* book and lend it to me. I always return it to her unread.

I know she is right. I also know her words are not limited to my behaviour with Martin. They apply generally. They apply to Dorothy.

There was no exhilaration after my defiance, but later, sitting in the room that had once been the room I shared with Frances and then my room, I saw the piles of scrapbooks in the corner and I felt a renewed faith in what I had done. I could not have read the newspapers to her; I could not have done it.

*But this is not to say that I did not have my doubts,* I would have said to Jocelyn if I could have talked to her about what had happened. *There is no real harm in it and she needed help.*

It was just that I could not do it.

But I do not talk to Jocelyn about what has happened. I do not talk to anyone.

I bring Dorothy her food and she does not speak.

I clear her plate and she does not speak.

175

I wish her goodnight and close the door to her room. Still she does not speak.

The next morning it is as I expected. I am greeted with silence.

*You are pushing me*, I whisper to myself in the bathroom mirror, watching my mouth forming the words, tasting them on the tip of my tongue. *Pushing me, pushing me, pushing me.*

I open the curtains in her room, open them wide, letting the light spill in, particles of dust dancing across the carpet, across the veneer of her dressing-table, in front of the mirror and in front of the photograph of Franco.

I can see the fury on my mother's face as she squints in the unaccustomed brightness of daylight.

*I am going to work*, I tell her and she does not answer. I take her breakfast tray and notice she has eaten everything. I straighten her bed covers and ask her if she would like me to brush her hair.

She does not say a word.

In the corridor, I lean against the wall, close my eyes and breathe deeply. I do not have the stomach for this.

*You should pack and move while he is away*, Jocelyn said to me yesterday when I told her about Martin.

It is easy for her to say this. She does not know the place to which I would have to return.

*He is not good for you*, she said. *I saw him with his wife and I have seen him with you. He likes to keep people repressed. To make himself feel better.*

I wanted to tell her she was wrong. He is good for me, I wanted to say. I wanted to tell her about the afternoon he had held me at the end of the jetty. I wanted to tell her that he has seen things and knows things about me no one else knows. And he is still with me, I wanted to say.

And I wanted to say that I could not go back. Not to this place.

But I did not say a word.

*I will help you*, she promised. *Just tell me when.*

I open my eyes to the dimness of this corridor, to the yellowing paint and to the faded print of an English garden, dull behind dirty glass.

She expects me to have a courage I do not have.

Outside, the morning is clear and clean. The next-door neighbour scrubs her flyscreen door with a toothbrush and in the house beyond that, a man mows his lawn. I am late, but I do not move. At the top of the back steps I look out past the Hills Hoist and the back fence to the houses on the other side of the road. I can almost see as far as John Mills's. Almost but not quite.

I remember standing on the hilltop at Marissa's, Martin once again speaking for me. *Poor Elise grew up with a pebbled back yard. I don't think she had seen a flower until she moved in with me.*

I remember his words and my cheeks sting.

It is then that I make up my mind.

*I am sorry,* I tell David, the General Manager, on the telephone. *I need a few days off.*

I explain that Dorothy is ill, that there is no one to care for her, and as I lie, I can hear her, coughing in her room, coughing loudly to let me know she is listening to every word I am saying.

*I will be back next week*, I promise him.

He tells me to take as long as I need. *We'll manage*, he reassures me.

I open the door to Dorothy's room and the brightness startles me. I tell her I am going out.

Her coughing has stopped. She is, once again, silent.

*Do you need anything?* I ask her, knowing there is no point. She will not answer.

I close the door behind me and leave her lying flat on her back staring up at the ceiling.

# 31

*It was you who gave me the inspiration,* I tell him. *Indirectly,* I add.

John Mills is sitting on the back steps when I come home and he watches, with surprise, as the taxi driver and I bring in bags of soil, compost and straw, a load of plants, and the sparkling new rake I selected.

When I moved into Martin's mother's house and told him I wanted to plant vegetables, he was surprised. *I really don't want to dig up the lawn,* he said, *or any of the beds,* and he looked out the back window at the buffalo grass and the row of crimson roses, bruised and wilted in the heat. *Besides,* he added, *this is low maintenance.*

I did not argue. It was not my house. But it did not stop me wanting.

*I was thinking about your mosaic,* I tell John, as he helps me drag the bags to the back steps. *I was thinking about you covering the garden with china, and I wished that I could cover this.* I point to the pebbles, all of them, colourless at our feet. *And then I remembered.*

He wipes the sheen of sweat from his forehead and takes his glasses off, resting them next to his sketchbook. He has been drawing. The pages flap in the breeze, covering this morning's picture.

*I remembered the seaweed. And all the newspaper,* I tell him.

I remembered Marissa explaining how she had built up her garden. Standing in the clear heat of that summer day and listening to her speak.

*A layer of seaweed, a layer of newspaper, and then straw and earth,* I say to John.

I point to the back fence, rusty and twisted, and to the northern side of the yard. *You can lay it straight on top of the pebbles,* I tell him, remembering how amazed I had been when she had told me. She had pointed to the rocky outcrops of quartz that surrounded us, pink and cream, like the cliffs on the beach. *The soil is stony here,* she had told me, *and rather than dig it all up, I decided to try this.*

To grow something on top of stone had seemed inconceivable to me.

It still does.

John Mills looks at the lettuces and herbs I have bought and, at our feet, the packets of seeds, promising poppies, sunflowers and foxgloves, bright and colourful, spread out on the cracked concrete.

*And sweet corn,* I tell him.

*Why not?* he says and, picking up the packet, he reads the instructions on the back.

I tell him my plan.

The seaweed is first. I will collect it from the beach and wash it down to get rid of the salt. I point to the stack of newspapers in the sunroom.

*More than enough*, he says.

The straw and the compost are in the bags at our feet.

*And I'll border the beds with the pebbles,* I tell him, still surprised at how possible it all is.

*Have you told Dorothy?* he asks me, and I look at the ground.

I tell him I want it to be a surprise.


Later, at the beach, we walk along together, dragging our bags of seaweed behind us.

John Mills tells me about his wife.

*I loved her*, he says. *We were lucky.*

I do not remember her well. She worked in the surgery with him and I met her once. The time I went to him with measles. But the memory is vague.

He retired soon after she died.

*I had been disillusioned for a long time*, he says. *It all felt so useless. Most of the time people just wanted to talk. I always felt I could do more without all the trappings, all the pretence, of the surgery but I couldn't bring myself to let them go.*

*She was the catalyst. She didn't want to try anything; chemotherapy, radiotherapy. She said she wanted to die in peace.*

*And that was so hard for me to accept.*

I steal a glance at him.

181

*I fought her and I wish I hadn't.*

He pauses for a moment, and I wait for him to continue. *It was something I had to come to terms with,* he says, and he looks out across the calm blue of the sea. *The mosaic is my peace offering; that and my daily rounds,* and he turns to me. *That is all they are,* he says, *a way of finding peace.*

At home, we lay the seaweed out on the pebbles, flat beneath the warmth of the winter sun.

He sprays it down with the hose. One side at a time. I turn it over. It is slimy to the touch.

*I'm not so sure about this part of the process,* he says.

*Neither am I,* I admit, as I run my hands along the knots of weed to check whether we have washed away most of the salt.

We are hungry and he makes lunch. He takes a sandwich in to Dorothy and brings one out for me.

*I'll stay out here,* I tell him, assuming that he will, as always, go and eat with her.

I sit by myself and look out across the yard, the thick clumps of weed drying in the sun.

When I told Martin about Marissa's garden, he had not understood why I was so excited.

*It's just a garden,* he had said to me.

When I told him about John Mills's mosaic, he also did not understand.

*Fifteen years,* he said. *How can anything take that long?* and he shook his head in disbelief.

We are different, Martin and I. Very different. In my moments of honesty, I can see that the differences are fundamental and there is little likelihood of this changing.

After lunch, I begin work on the borders. With the largest pebbles, I mark the shape of the beds, building higher with the smaller stones. I am finished by the time John comes out and we stand together and look at the progress I have made.

*Not bad*, he says, *not bad at all*.

We lay the seaweed, piece by piece, tangled green, yellow and black, across the remaining pebbles that line the base of the beds.

The newspaper is next, and I am momentarily daunted by the size of the piles in the sunroom. I start with the stack closest to the door; the paper is not so old, not so yellowed as the bundles in the corners, and I carry armfuls down the back steps to John, who lays them across the layers of seaweed.

It is like shedding skin, I think to myself, but I do not say it out loud because I know that my analogy is not a clear one. It is just a sense.

The sun has moved to the front of the house, and the evening chill is upon us. The nights still come early and I know we will not be able to finish before dark. I drag the bags of straw and compost to each of the beds and empty them, wanting to at least see the earth covering the pebbles before I stop for the day.

John helps me. He rakes the straw, and then the soil, until the covering is even, and finally we rest.

*I remember the first flower I grew*, he says to me. We are standing at the gate, looking at the work we have done and the red of the sky over the rooftops. *It was a sunflower. I watched it open up. Half the petals unfolded,*

183

*the other half stayed tightly closed against the centre. Hiding half its face.* He smiles. *I was intrigued. I had never seen this slow unfolding before.*

As he speaks, I can imagine.

*I will see you tomorrow*, he says, and I watch him head down the street until I cannot see him any more. He has left me, alone with Dorothy and her silence.

I walk up the back steps and I am tired. The house is in darkness, so I do not see that I have left the photo out. Not straight away. Not until I have checked on Dorothy and come back into the kitchen to make her dinner.

I switch on the light and it is there. In the middle of the table. Next to the breadboard where he made our sandwiches. Where I left it last night, forgetting to hide it as I normally would. Leaving it out. For anyone to see.

He could not have missed it.

And I hold it with the tips of my fingers and feel uneasy.

He must have seen it and yet he did not say a word.

# 32

*Was she like you?* Martin asked me on the night I first told him about Frances.

I was silent.

In the darkness I could not see his face. I could not see his eyes, his nose or his mouth, and I could not answer him.

No, she was not like me. But they were not the words I spoke.

*Not so different*, I said, shifting uneasily in the small space next to him, wanting to see his face but knowing that when I did it would be the face of a stranger, and closing my eyes because ultimately to see nothing had seemed easier.

No, she was not so different.

Not as different as he had seemed in the darkness of that room.

And that night when Martin made love to me, I kept

my face turned from his and, with my eyes closed, I tried to remember another time. I tried to remember kissing the Polish boy outside the Chinese Palace restaurant with the seagulls circling overhead.

But it was no use.

The branches of the olive tree scratched against the window and I could not escape where I was.

Sometimes I wonder whether he, too, closed his eyes and pretended he was with someone else. He kissed me, but was he kissing his wife, or perhaps his first girlfriend?

I do not know. We never talked about those things.

*Why did she leave you?* I asked him once, looking at the photograph of her in his mother's lounge room.

He scratched his arm (this is what he does when he is ill at ease) and told me he did not want to talk about it.

*Besides*, he said, *she did not leave me. We both decided*, and he scratched his arm again. *It was mutual*.

But I knew he was lying.

Jocelyn has told me that they fought all the time. She has also told me that she ran off with someone else.

And soon after, he met me.

Someone who would listen. Someone who would not run away.

Martin believes there are certain subjects that should not be discussed.

*These things should be private*, he says, referring to Jocelyn's talk of old lovers, men she has slept with and men she has wanted to sleep with.

He tells me he is glad I am not like her, spilling intimate details to whomever will listen.

186

He is right. I am not like her. But then, apart from the Polish boy, there has never been anyone but Martin.

*How would she like it*, he says, *if they all talked about her in the way she talks about them?*

*She probably wouldn't mind*, I say, but so softly he does not hear me.

*I'm sure she would hate it,* he says. *I know I would, and I certainly wouldn't subject someone I have loved to the public scrutiny she indulges in.*

I wonder whether I will become a topic Martin refuses to discuss. I wonder whether my photo will be left out, along with the photo of his wife, side by side, for the next one to look at. I wonder whether she will ask him about me and whether he will scratch his arm nervously and tell her he does not want to talk about it. Or perhaps she will banish both of us, the wife and me, to some box in a cupboard, not needing evidence of the past to reaffirm the present.

I do not know.

There may not even be a photograph.

I may simply cease to exist. I will pack my box and my clothes and, neither mentioned nor displayed, I will disappear.

*I will help you*, Jocelyn said to me. *Just tell me when.*

I know I have not moved from his house. I know I have not done what he has asked.

But there was a time when Martin told me he would never leave me. Years ago, when he thought I was someone else. Encircling me in his arms at the end of the jetty, I could not explain why I could not walk out there as he had wanted, and he had told me it was all right.

*I will look after you. Always.*

I will look after you. Always.

I cannot explain what those words meant to me.

Outside it is cold and clear. There is a full moon, heavy and yellow, and it hangs low in the sky. So low that it is possible to see each pebble bordering the beds I marked out today, smooth and distinct.

Down the street, the face of John Mills's wife glitters back at the stars.

And somewhere, miles away, Martin sleeps.

# 33

*Doing a bit of gardening?* The next-door neighbour looks at me from across the fence. Like me, she is on the top of the back steps, but unlike the steps I stand on, hers are not cracked cement and they are not covered in newspapers.

I smile at her and turn quickly in the hope this will stop her from talking.

But it doesn't.

*How is she?* She nods her head in the direction of the house, and I tell her that Dorothy is fine. On the mend.

*If there's anything I can do*, she offers, and I thank her, one foot already inside the door.

She shrugs her shoulders and goes back to what she was doing, on her hands and knees, scrubbing the grouting between the already pristine tiles.

*She's mad*, Dorothy once said to me. *I have never seen a woman clean like she cleans.*

I resisted the temptation to tell her that she probably

uses the same word to describe her. Mad. Although I doubt she would call my mother a fanatic cleaner.

This morning I do not open Dorothy's curtains. I put the papers by the side of her bed, the pile already mounting to an unmanageable height, and leave her in the darkness she prefers. She does not speak to me and I do not speak to her. Today I do not have the heart to try.

This silence is not new. I have lived it before and I know she can last beyond the point where most people would turn back.

*She is not talking*, Frances would say, loudly and clearly, and right in front of her.

Dorothy would not flinch.

Often the silence was directed at Frances alone, but sometimes I, too, would find myself caught within it, smothered by it. It would descend upon us and I would retreat, unable to fight it, while Frances kept on talking.

*Fuck it*, Frances would say, relishing the word, and she would reach for one of Dorothy's cigarettes and light it, slowly, purposefully, right in front of her. *Want one?* She would push the pack towards me and I would shake my head, giggling nervously at how far Frances was prepared to go.

Dorothy would not even look at us.

*Well, I'm off*, and Frances would slam the back door behind her. *Don't know when I'll be back*, and she would be gone, leaving the two of us alone. Silent in this house.

But not all the silences were directed at us. Some were more general. They were not a punishment. They were a complete retreat.

When Franco died, Dorothy did not speak for a fortnight, not to us, not to anyone.

I remember going to the parklands for Frances's birthday, five days after we had been told the news. We sat by the banks of the river that twists green and murky through this city, where the paddleboats are tied up ready to be hired. I stayed on the grass with Dorothy, watching Frances and her friends paddle up and down, screaming at each other, trying to drive their boats into each other, Frances eventually jumping over the side of hers and into the water below. When the man came and asked Dorothy to keep an eye on them, when he suggested they were making a nuisance of themselves and that someone could get hurt, she did not respond. She just glanced up at him, squinting in the bright sunlight, and smiled vaguely.

Eventually, he gave up, looking at me with a concern that filled me with shame. I could not explain that it was not him, it did not have anything to do with what he had said, it was just the way things were. It was just the way she was.

But that silence was different. It was not like this one.

This one has a purpose. I know what she wants from me and I do not know how long I can hold out. I do not know if I have the strength. Because there is not just her, and there is not just Martin and me; now there is him, too. John Mills. He will be here soon and I do not want to see him. I do not want to see him, knowing that he has seen. My photograph. Left on the kitchen table.

I do not even tell her I am going for a walk. I close the

gate behind me and I head towards the beach, past the rows of dilapidated bungalows, eaten away by the salt air that slowly peels back paint, leaving walls and verandah posts naked and raw. I can smell the freshness of the sea before I even come over the rise at the end of the street and see it stretching for miles, flat and still under the crispness of this blue sky.

This is the best time of year.

The last breath of winter in the air and the promise of summer ahead.

Jim Hunt is out the front of the kiosk, sweeping the cement that surrounds the shop. The roller door is pulled up and the signs are out. Ice-creams, hot pies, fish, chips. He looks up at me and nods as I pass.

I look away.

Jim Cunt, the older boys used to call him.

*A bloody perve*, Frances used to say.

The plastic ribbons would swing in the afternoon sea breeze, multi-coloured, flicking back and forth, flick flack flick, and I would hold my bottle of Woodies up high over the counter and push the money across to him, pulling my hand back so that I did not have to touch him, not those fingers, long and yellow with dirt under the nails.

He would give me extra change. *For your pretty green eyes.*

I would leave the money behind. Always.

Jim Cunt.

*An ice-cream for a quick grope. You know what I mean?*

Two little girls run past. Long blonde hair in ponytails

192

that swing like a streak of light in the brilliance of the morning. A flash of legs and a swish of tartan skirts as they head towards the path down to the beach.

*Wait*, the shorter one calls out, but her friend does not stop and she runs, stumbling across the cracked bitumen to catch up.

*You can't get me*, and she can't. She falls, her skirt flipping up, a shocked howl as she slams down hard on the pavement outside the kiosk.

It is then that I see him watching. Jim Hunt, watching as her friend runs back and bends down, hand outstretched to where the other lies. He does not move, still as the brick pillar behind him.

The friend also sees him, sees his eyes on the flipped-up skirt and the small blue cotton underpants underneath, and she brushes the skirt down quickly before pulling her up.

*Come on*, and she yanks at her hand, looking nervously back at him. *Quick,* and she pulls her away from the direction in which they had been heading, putting distance between them and the dirty old man.

I, too, no longer want to go to the beach.

I, too, turn my back on him and head towards the road, no longer wanting to walk, suddenly wanting to go home.

When I get back to Dorothy's house, John Mills is, as I had expected, already there.

I can hear him from in the kitchen. He is in her room and he is reading to her. Just the headlines and the first few paragraphs, punctuated by her voice telling him to stop, *Yes, that one,* and the slice of the scissors as he clips the article for her.

I do not want to know.

*No planting today?* he asks when he comes out and finds me reading on the back steps.

I shake my head, but I do not look at him. I do not want to give him an opportunity to speak.

He lowers himself carefully onto the step above mine and stretches his legs out in front of him.

*But no going back to work?* he asks.

I tell him I need a bit of time. *To think about things,* I say.

He nods and we are silent.

*She seems a little better.* He tries to open up the conversation again. *She is not in so much pain.*

Still staring out at the garden we have begun to make, I tell him she is not speaking to me. Hasn't for a couple of days. In my fingers, I have a leaf of the mint I bought yesterday and I am rolling it into a tiny ball. I flick it out across the remaining pebbles and watch to see where it lands.

He does not know what to say.

*She's not well.* He knows as well as I do that that is not the reason but he says it anyway.

*Can I get you a cup of tea?* and he leans forward to touch me, lightly, on the shoulder.

I wish he wouldn't.

I shake my head and tell him I am fine.

He seems about to say something else and then decides against it.

I know I should speak. I know I should say something of the photograph he must have seen but I can't.

Together we stare out across the yard and I think of those little girls.

The two of them, running across the car park and down towards the beach.

# 34

Dorothy drives badly. She drives without looking where she is going. She drives without thinking about whether she should accelerate or brake but lets her feet just move on the pedals of their own accord. She turns corners without indicating. She does not say a word.

I sit in the back, holding the door handle, fighting an irresistible urge to let my body fling from side to side with the movement of the car, because I know Dorothy would turn around and slap me. I do not really know why I want to do this, it just feels like the right response to this high-speed drama. Racing through the night-time streets to the police station with the windows open and the wind rushing, rushing through the car.

It is not far, only a few blocks, but when we pull up at the front, I feel ill. Carsick with a steady nausea that thickens at the bottom of my stomach and threatens to slowly rise, but I push it back down, deep down, knowing that this is not the time or the place to cry out, *I want to be sick.*

It is Dorothy who leads the way, the heels of her sandals click-clacking on the four tiled steps that lead up to the front door and into a small and dingy corridor that is plastered with notices, *Wanted* and *Missing.* I scan them all in the one brief instant before we turn into the reception area, and I cannot help but imagine Frances's face on all of them. Wanted and Missing. Both.

There is a man at the reception desk. He has come to pick up his wallet, but he does not have his identification number with him, and the policewoman is irritated.

*I cannot give it back to you,* she says, her voice clipped and sharp, *without the number.*

*Jesus,* and the man slams his fist down. *I have to go all the way home, get it and then come all the way back again?*

*Yes,* and the policewoman does not flinch, but turns slowly, purposefully, to where Dorothy waits, fidgeting with her car keys at the other end of the counter.

*Can I help you?* she asks, her voice polite but crisp.

I am holding my breath, waiting for my mother to speak. I do not know what she is going to say, and suddenly the way in which she intends to define the situation is important. The policewoman also leans forward, waiting to hear.

*Is there something wrong?* she asks, because Dorothy is silent. There is a slight sheen of sweat across her forehead because it is hot in here, hot and stuffy, the only relief coming from a single electric fan that rickets around overhead. Slowly.

*It is my daughter,* Dorothy says, and both the police-woman and I lean closer. *She hasn't come home.*

*You want to report her missing?*

Dorothy hesitates: *No,* and then changes her mind. *I mean, yes,* and I let myself breathe again. So that is what it is. Missing. I can see the poster already. I want to take my mother's hand, but Dorothy has both hands up on the counter. Still playing with her keys. Running them round and round the metal ring.

*When did you last see her?*

*This morning,* and Dorothy brushes her hair back from her face, where it falls, tangled and thick in her eyes.

*And she hasn't gone to a friend's?*

*I don't know. I don't think so.*

Perhaps we have made a mistake, been overanxious, and I glance at Dorothy and see that she, too, is doubting.

*If you'll come this way,* and the policewoman lifts up the counter and leads us into a small room just off the reception area, *I'll call the sergeant.*

We wait, seated side by side.

*Don't.* Dorothy glares at me.

I am kicking at the leg of the chair without realising what I am doing. Thump, thump, thump. I stop and sit perfectly still, hands in my lap. I have never been in a police station before. Once, about a year ago, when Frances got caught shoplifting, Dorothy came down to pick her up. I had to wait at home until they both returned, stony-faced and silent.

The sergeant closes the door behind him and sits down heavily in the large chair on the other side of the desk. He introduces himself and starts with the preliminary questions: Frances's name, age and our address. I listen as Dorothy answers. There is a poster above the desk. Road safety week, a cartoon cat at a crossing, bright-coloured stripes.

*Right,* and the sergeant leans back in his chair and crosses his arms behind his head. The preliminaries are over. *So when did you last see,* and he looks at his notes, *Frances?*

*This morning.* Dorothy lights a cigarette. *But Elise,* and she jerks her head in my direction, *saw her after that.*

The sergeant has blue eyes. Brilliant blue. And thick black hair. He leans closer and smiles. *And when did you last see your sister?* His voice is cigarette husky and slow. He is coaxing me. He can see I am nervous and do not know where the words are.

*This morning.*

*Can you tell me a little bit about where you were and what you were doing?*

Hot crimson in my cheeks, I try to tell him: walking to the beach, the usual way, stopping near the path through the dunes, the usual spot, making arrangements, and then waiting.

Waiting.

In the rock pool, under the fierce blue sky.

I do not know what else to say.

*Did you go and look for her anywhere?*

The jetty. I forgot about the jetty.

*That's all right,* and the sergeant smiles kindly, encouragingly, at me.

Dorothy butts out her cigarette. She, too, waits for me to speak.

The boys. Long skinny legs in tight black jeans, and Johnno grins at me but I just don't know what type of grin it is. Backed up against the railing. Thrusting the skinny boy's jeans into his hands and not being able to bear to look at him and see that gratitude. *Have any of you seen my sister Frances?* Did I ask or was I too shy to speak? I cannot remember.

*That's all right,* the sergeant says again. *If we need to we'll go and chat to them ourselves.* He takes down a few more notes.

Dorothy lights another cigarette.

*Was there anything at all unusual you noticed about Frances this morning?*

Dorothy shakes her head.

The sergeant turns to me.

Nothing.

*Was she taking extra things with her when you left? Did she seem nervous? Anxious? Was there anything you noticed that struck you as being different?*

I am searching, pick pick picking through everything I can remember, wanting to find it, something, anything to hang on to. Frances in her new bikini that she nicked from Grace Brothers last week, her shorts, her towel, no bag; but I cannot really remember because I had seen no need to notice. That is the problem. If only I had known.

Dorothy is agitated. One leg jiggling up and down, she

puts her cigarette out and interrupts. *Can I just call home?* she asks. *She may be back by now.*

The sergeant pushes the phone towards her, and we both watch as Dorothy dials, as Dorothy waits, hand gripping the receiver, for an answer. Nothing.

*Okay,* the sergeant says. *The best thing would be for you both to go home and wait. If she hasn't returned by morning, I want you to call the duty sergeant first thing.*

We nod our heads in agreement and when he stands to leave, we do too. There does not seem to be anything else to do. But just as we are pushing our chairs back into place, side by side, he stops us.

One more question.

*I'm sorry to have to ask this, Mrs Silverton*, and Dorothy looks up at him, eyes wide and startled, *but has there been any kind of trouble at home? Anything that could have made her want to run away?*

Has there been?

*Nothing. No.* She shakes her head vehemently in response. *Never*, she adds. *She's my little girl. My baby.*

Don't start. Please don't start.

*What about her father? Do he and Frances get along?*

*They love each other.*

I look up at Dorothy in surprise.

She corrects herself. *Franco, I mean, her father, is dead. He has been for some time.*

*I'm sorry*, the sergeant says, *very sorry. It must be difficult for you on your own.*

Dorothy does not answer and he is awkward, unsure as to whether he should comfort her or let her be. He

201

looks anxiously out to the other room, wanting to catch the policewoman's eye. *Shall we get you a cup of tea before you leave?*

Dorothy shakes her head and turns to the door.

*Call us,* he says, *if you hear anything, if she comes back,* and he sees us out to the reception area.

Dorothy is walking quickly and I am struggling to keep up with her. I look back to say goodbye but he has already gone and I have to run down the stairs and across the car park to catch up with Dorothy, who is already in the car, key in the ignition.

She does not turn to look at me as I get into the back seat.

*Will they find her?* I ask, but she does not answer.

And as we drive home in silence, I stare out the window and I go through the policeman's questions.

And I wonder, just for a moment, about that last one. About the trouble at home.

# 35

In the late afternoon, the telephone rings.

John Mills has gone, and the sound of the ringing is sharp and harsh in the quiet of this house.

I answer, hoping it will be Martin, but it is not his voice that speaks to me. It is Jocelyn's.

She is calling to find out how I am. She is calling to see if there is anything she can do. And she is calling to remind me that tonight is her exhibition opening and I had promised I would come.

*It will do you good,* she tells me, *to get out. Even if it is only for a short while.*

I do not want to go. I put the phone down and wish I had managed to be more forceful. But each time I had tried to make an excuse, she had stopped me.

The gallery is to the south of the parklands. I have to catch the number 12 into the city and then another bus out again, past the gardens where couples marry in the spring, taking their vows by the pavilion before posing for photographs on the bridge that spans this section of the river. In winter the parklands are green, in summer they are burnt to a brown dust, with only patches surviving the heat, the constant watering of a few spots ensuring a smattering of green in the thick brown belt that encircles this city.

During the day, people stroll through these parklands. In the early evening they are empty.

They are not a place where you would want to be. Not at night. Not on your own.

And I stare into them from the safety of the bus window. Trying to see in there, right in there, where it is only black before my eyes.

The gallery is in the first suburb beyond the city centre.

When I arrive, I can hear the opening before I turn the corner and see it. People spill out the door and on to the street and I do not know why she said she wanted me to come.

I am about to turn around and make my escape, I am about to disappear without even saying hello, when I catch her eye, and it is too late. She is leaning against the door, a beer in one hand and a cigarette in the other. She is leaning close to a man I recognise from the theatre. An actor who was in a play last season. She is laughing loudly at something he has said, and I am about to keep walking, thinking she has not seen me, when she calls out my name, high and clear, from across the street.

*Elise*, and she moves through the crowd towards me, unsteady on the heels she has borrowed for the occasion.

*Elise*, and she hugs me, her coat warm against my cheek, the sweet smell of beer on her breath.

*I did not expect to see you*, she says, and she leads me back through the crush of people towards the entrance. *It is not as crowded as it looks,* she says. *It is just that everyone comes outside to smoke*, and she lights another cigarette herself.

The man she had been talking to nods briefly at me and I nod back at him.

*Go inside and tell me what you think,* Jocelyn urges me. *I'd really like to know.*

As I step into the brightness of the gallery, I hear her telling him that I am someone she works with. *On the box office*, she says.

Jocelyn's work skirts the edge of the room, and I follow it, walking from piece to piece by myself. In the harsh light, I feel self-conscious. I am aware of my solitude. I hold my program tight in one hand and a glass of wine in the other. I am staring at each nude intently, without really seeing any of them at all.

*Do you like it?* Jocelyn asks me when I have come full circle.

I tell her that I do, but I would like to see it again.

She is drunk now and she squeezes my hand. She asks me if I have heard from Martin and I tell her I haven't. I can see she is about to offer me some words of encouragement, some words to spur me on to do what she knows I should do, and I do not want to hear them. She leans close to me in an attempt to be heard above the noise that surrounds us and tells me she is still happy to help. *We can put your stuff in my ute*, she says and I thank her, but she has already been distracted by someone else who is congratulating her as he leaves.

I, too, turn to the door, but she stops me.

*You're not leaving already are you?* and she clutches my arm. *You've met Marissa?* and she puts her other hand on the sleeve of the woman standing next to her.

We look at each other.

I would not have recognised her.

I doubt she would have recognised me.

We both smile and say that yes we have, we have met before, and turn back to Jocelyn for help, but she is talking to someone else.

*How are you?* Marissa asks, and I tell her I am well.

*And Martin? You are still with Martin?*

I am about to say yes I am. I am about to say he is well too, but I find I can't. I do not know what to say.

*He is away*, I tell her. *We are having a break*.

She smiles, and I do not think she has heard me. *Well, nice to see you again,* she says, and she reaches for Jocelyn across the crowd of people that now separates us.

*I have to go too,* I tell her, mouthing the words as she makes her way back towards us.

She asks me how I am getting home and when I tell her the bus, she turns to Marissa.

I know what is coming next and I am dreading it.

*Aren't you staying at the beach?* Jocelyn asks and, as I had feared, Marissa says she is, in the next suburb along; of course she can take me. No trouble at all.

Marissa drives an old black Volkswagen.

She throws papers and clothes onto the back seat in an attempt to clear a space for me in the chaos that seems to fill the car.

*The heater doesn't work*, she tells me as she puts on gloves and a scarf. *Nor does the demister*, and she opens the window to let in the chill of the night. Our breath is frosty in this small space, and I watch the icy puffs that accompany each of her words.

We talk briefly about Jocelyn's work, and she tells me that she found it slightly immature.

*But that's Jocelyn*, she says.

I ask her about her own paintings.

She tells me she has had a difficult time. She is no longer living with Robert and she has been deciding whether she should leave the house. It makes it difficult to paint, she tells me, and I nod in sympathy as she talks.

She speaks more quickly than I remembered, her words tumbling out in long rapid sentences as she tells me it has been a time of reassessing her life. She had wanted a child, she says, and he had told her that he couldn't. Not yet. *But now he is*, she laughs, *with his new girlfriend. You think you have it all*, and she rubs at the windscreen with her sleeve, *and then it is remarkable how quickly it can all disintegrate.*

She asks me again how Martin is and this time I do not hesitate. *I think we are splitting up*, I say and she laughs.

*What do you mean? Believe me, when you're splitting up, you know*, and she looks across at me. But she is not really interested. She just keeps talking, wanting to tell me all of it, everything; her words do not stop, punctuated only by her continual wiping of the windscreen, fogging in the cold.

She is not the person I remembered.

I had once wanted to be like her. Just like her. But she is not the person I remembered.

*I am sorry*, she says as we pull up outside Dorothy's house. *I haven't shut up. It has just been hard.*

She is looking down at her lap as she speaks, picking at a loose thread in her gloves.

*It will be okay,* I say, wanting to comfort her but not knowing how.

*I know*, and she starts up the engine again, revving on the accelerator, uncomfortable in the silence that has descended. *Good to see you*, and she waves at me out the window. She is anxious to get going. *Send my love to Martin*, and she toots the horn as she pulls back out into the darkness of this street and drives off.

I am left with one hand on the back gate, and as I look at the beds I have prepared, I remember the Marissa who had shown me her garden. All those years ago.

*You think you have it all.*

And I had thought she had. I remember.

Tomorrow I will plant, I tell myself. I will plant because it is something I have always wanted. Just for me. And I must keep going.

# 36

It is, as I had hoped, a perfect morning.

I have spread out the pots of lettuces, spinach and herbs across the pebbles in front of me, and I am watering them, squinting in the dazzle of clear morning light that makes the spray from the hose glitter before my eyes, when John Mills arrives.

I look up in surprise when I hear the rusty squeak of the gate as it swings shut behind him.

He is earlier than usual.

He asks me whether there has been any improvement, unsure of how to phrase the question, but I understand what it is he wants to know. He wants to know whether Dorothy is now talking to me.

Last night, when I came in from the gallery, I washed her down in the way he had told me. I sponged her with warm soapy water, across the blotched softness of her skin, neither of us able to look at each other. She did not speak and I did not try. We simply performed the task that had to be done, trying to pretend that that was all it was, a task, and not an intimacy that felt all the more uncomfortable in the silence that enclosed us.

*No, there has not been any improvement*, I say, hating the fact I am using his words.

He is awkward. *She is not talking?*

*No,* I tell him, *not a word.*

I take her breakfast into her while he waits in the kitchen. She is propped up in the bed, her hair loose around her shoulders, and I brush it quickly for her, untangling the ends before twisting it on top of her head.

When I come back, he is sitting at the table as I left him. *Have you asked her why she is doing this?*

I tell him there is no point. Apart from the fact that she would not answer me, I already know the reason. I know why.

*Perhaps if you told her you found it upsetting?* he suggests.

He knows her well, but he does not seem to know her in the way I do.

I watch him as he traces a circle on the table with his finger and, for a man who is usually so calm and meas-ured, it is an action of agitation.

*I'll go and chat to her*, he says, and he sees the alarm on my face. *Don't worry*, he reassures me, *I will be careful*.

I tell him there is no need. It will be all right eventu-ally, although, in my heart, I fear it is conceivable that this silence could continue indefinitely. I cannot imagine how it could break, but I do not say this out loud.

*I am going to check on her anyway*, he says, and he takes his cup of tea with him.

I listen as he knocks on her door, tapping gently before pushing it open. I hear him go in and I do not want to hear any more.

Out in the yard, I do not want to think about Dorothy. I do not want to think about him and the photograph that is still unmentioned. I do not want to think about any of them. I water the beds I have made, slowly, thoroughly, letting the water soak into the rich brown soil, and I plan where I will position each of my plants. I am lost in rows of sunflowers and foxgloves, and I do not hear him as he comes out on to the back steps and across the pebbles towards me.

*She says she is tired*, and I know he has not talked to her in the way he wanted.

In his hand, he is carrying a brown envelope. *I brought these to show you*, he says. *I developed them last night,* and he hands the envelope to me.

My fingers are damp and I wipe them on the edge of my shirt.

*Perhaps we should sit on the steps,* he suggests.

I want to plant while it is still cool, before the winter sun rises high overhead, but I do not say this to him. I follow him without a word.

*I haven't used the darkroom for months*, he says.

I did not know he even had one.

He tells me he set it up in his doctor's surgery after he retired. *I packed up the room and locked the door behind me. I remember thinking it was yet another room I would*

211

*not use now that Ingrid had died. And the thought depressed me.*

The envelope is unsealed. I lift the flap and feel the prints inside. Cool and glossy beneath my fingers.

*It was Will who suggested it. We laughed about how dark and gloomy the room was and he suggested putting it to use. So we stacked all the files in the corner and remodelled the rest. A doctor's surgery no more.*

I lay the prints out on the step in front of me, his words only half heard as I look down at them, and it is not easy, at first, to see what they are.

The stripe of washed-up seaweed. Both fascinating and repulsive; I hear those words as he spoke them then, that grey Sunday morning. A black and oily stripe across harsh white sand.

I do not know why he is showing them to me.

*They are good,* I tell him, and I move slightly, edging myself up and back to the planting, catching his eye accidentally.

He is, as I had anticipated, about to speak, and I do not know if I want to hear.

I pick up the pot of herbs closest to my feet. I want to plant it in the bed that borders the side fence, near the back door.

*Please,* he says, *we need to talk,* and he rubs the side of his face with the palm of his hand, looking down at the steps.

*Do you remember,* he asks me, *do you remember that night? That night you came and got me? The night she disappeared?*

I do, and I nod my head in silence as I begin to make a small hole in the bed at my feet.

I remember it well, and I am afraid of what is going to come next.

# 37

The house is empty.

I know it before we even reach the back door.

A light burns, yellow and harsh, in the kitchen. We can see it from the gate. But it is only the light we left on before we went to the police and it does not fool either of us. Because the rest of the house is dark. Completely dark, and we know she is not home.

I stare up at the sky while Dorothy searches for her key. The night is clear and I can see stars. Hundreds of them, perhaps thousands, shimmering above me. *Some of them are so far away that they do not exist any more. All we are seeing is their light from years ago,* Frances once said and I had not understood. I still don't.

*And there are so many of them that it is possible that one of them is an exact duplication of our life here. There is another city just like this one and in that city there is another beach the same as this and another house identical to ours and in that house there is another bedroom that belongs to two girls who are another Frances and Elise. Just like us.*

Just like us.

Dorothy opens the back door and I wonder whether the other Dorothy is doing exactly the same.

*Do they look exactly like we look?*

*Exactly.*

*Are they doing exactly what we are doing now?*

*Exactly.*

*Even asking the same question that I am asking, only they are asking it about us, right now?*

I cannot comprehend the enormity of it. I wonder whether the other Frances is also missing and wanted. Somewhere on that other planet, leaving that other Dorothy and Elise unsure of what to do or how to react. If I knew where the other Frances was then it would all be solved.

The kitchen smells of our dinner. Chop fat and soggy vegetables. I smell it as soon as Dorothy opens the door.

In that other kitchen, light years away, there is the same smell and that other Dorothy and Elise also stand, quiet and alone, looking at the dishes and pans in the sink and the red light of the clock on the windowsill.

Dorothy turns the water on. She turns the taps too far and it rushes out, splashing and spraying as it hits the stack of plates and glasses, roaring against the metal sink. Louder than I can bear. But she does not seem to notice. She just stands there, plug in hand as the spray dances around her, until eventually she realises, and she takes the dishes out of the sink, putting the plug in and letting it fill, soap bubbles rising, white and frothy, to the surface.

That other Dorothy also does not turn and look at her daughter. Not once. She just washes dishes, all her concentration now on the task in front of her, and she stacks the washed plates in the rack next to the sink. Today's dishes on top of yesterday's dishes.

I can see Frances's cereal bowl from breakfast, Frances's glass, her spoon, and I want to tell Dorothy to stop, to leave them, but I don't. Because it wouldn't make any sense. One by one they are plunged into the soapy water, and they emerge, no trace of Frances left.

It is late on the other planet. The clock in that kitchen near that beach in that city shows 10.45. Electric numbers like mean little red eyes. It is past the time the other Elise goes to bed and she is tired. But she does not want to go to her room. Not on her own. She waits near that other door and looks down that other corridor. It is dark in that other house. She wants to ask the other Dorothy to come with her and put her to bed.

*Good night,* I say.

*Good night,* the other Elise says in unison.

And together we head, frightened, for the room at the end of the hall, leaving the two Dorothys alone in their kitchens.

The door is closed. As I left it this afternoon. I try to shake the other Elise from my mind so that I alone can concentrate on what is happening here, now, in this world. I open the door and stand, in the darkness, trying to see.

216

My side of the room and Frances's side of the room. Mess on the floor and an unmade bed. I feel my way over, through the clothes, magazines and towels, twisted and strewn with no respect for the boundary we drew up, my eyes gradually becoming acclimatised to the dark.

Scared of the dark. But more scared of turning the light on and finding the bed is, as I expected, empty.

I sit on the floor and close my eyes until there is nothing but smell, and that smell is Frances; it is in the clothes that surround me, the unmade bed, the shoes tossed in the corner, all Frances. The Frances here, of this world. The Frances who is not here. I do not understand.

For Frances to sneak out is not unusual.

For Frances to be late is not unusual.

For Frances to be in trouble is not unusual.

But this. This is different.

There is not even an attempt to look as though she is keeping the rules. She has not come home at all. She has not done anything she was supposed to do.

And far away on that other planet, the other bed is also empty.

From the other end of the house, there is a smash.

I open my eyes.

It is just a plate dropping, clattering hard on the kitchen floor, but I sit upright, all senses on alert, and wait for what will follow. A momentary silence, followed by another crash. Louder this time. No accident.

I stand slowly, each limb alien and heavy, as I walk, pressed close to the wall, down the corridor and to the kitchen. Not wanting to witness what I know I will witness. And pressed tight against the doorframe, small and invisible, I see her. This Dorothy. Wild and furious. Wild as she has not been wild for years. Flinging plates, hurtling them, throwing them, across the kitchen to the wall. And they smash. Shatter. Fly out in a thousand china daggers.

*Stop,* I say, but I know I have not been heard. *Stop,* I try again. I block my ears and try to cover my eyes. I cannot bear it. Dorothy, white-faced, unaware of anything that falls outside the small and furious circle of her hysteria.

*Run,* Frances tells me. But it is not this Frances. It is the other one. *Get someone.*

And somewhere far away on another planet, the other Elise runs out the back gate and down that other street, where the pine trees also creak and the air smells salty and the road is cracked and potholed. She runs as fast as she can. Not knowing where she is heading until she is there. Knocking on his door.

# 38

John Mills puts the photographs back in the envelope. I can see him out of the corner of my eye.

*And you knocked loud enough to wake the dead*, he smiles.

Loud enough to wake the dead.

*At first I did not know who you were.*

No, he did not know who I was. I remember. He opened the door and I tried to tell him it was my mother, there was something wrong with my mother, but he could not hear me. My voice was too quiet.

I loosen the roots in the pot, shaking it slightly until I can feel the neat mould of soil coming away from the plastic that surrounds it. I am careful as I press it into the ground, gently patting the earth around it to make sure there are no pockets of air.

*I left you in the kitchen*, he says, *while I got changed.*

I remember, and I take the next pot of herbs, the mint, from the row at my feet.

He left me sitting at the table, and they were there, a pile of them.

The photographs.

I remember.

*I didn't even think of them*, he says. *I didn't even think you might find it strange that they were there. Not until sometime afterwards.*

I remember. He was getting changed in the laundry, asking me questions as he fumbled for clothes.

I do not want to talk about this. I do not want him to go on.

And as he asked those questions, Frances's face stared up at me from that pile of photographs, and my fingers were flicking through them, rummaging through them, aware of him just on the other side of the door, just managing to take the one, my one, and slip it into my pocket before he came out, T-shirt on back to front, tracksuit pants inside out.

He had his doctor's bag packed and ready and he picked it up with one hand, trying to take my hand with his other.

*We should walk*, he told me. *It will be quicker than getting the car out*, and I just nodded my head in agreement.

He asked me if something had happened to upset her and I could not answer him, even though I wanted to. I just nodded my head, up and down, up and down, and when he reached for my hand again, I pulled away.

I remember how quickly he walked, down the road that runs at the back of his house and at the back of our house, the road just there, over the gate. I had to run to keep up with him, but I did not ask him to slow down because I, too, wanted to get there as quickly as I could.

*It's here*, I told him when we reached our gate, and I remember both of us, running across these pebbles towards the back door.

*Mrs Silverton*, he called out, but there was no answer.

*Mrs Silverton*, he called again, and there was only silence.

We both stood, stunned, in the doorway. She had broken everything. Smashed it all.

*Mrs Silverton*, he called one more time and he was crossing the floor, china crunching under his shoes as he made his way to the other side of the room, calling out the whole time. Her name. Over and over.

I did not follow. Not even when I heard him find her, there in the lounge room. I just started picking up the pieces. The larger ones first. Half a plate, the handle of a cup, a saucepan, and I put them all, one by one, on the kitchen table.

*Elise*. It was him, and I stopped what I was doing. *Can you bring me a glass of water?*

I did not know whether there was a glass. At least, not an entire one. But there was. Forgotten, on top of the fridge, and I had to drag the chair over to reach it.

He was sitting with Dorothy in the lounge room. Her on the couch, him next to her with his arm around her. She had her head down in the palm of her hands and for one moment I thought she was crying, but then I realised she was not making a sound. All I could hear was his voice, on and on, soothing her, and he took the water from me without breaking his monologue. Telling her it would be all right. Over and over again. And he put the glass in her hand as he continued to talk. He put a couple of pills in the other hand, and he instructed her in the same voice to *Drink up now. Good, good, that will be better.*

Dorothy did as he said.

I remember.

I remember her face when she lifted her head to drink. It was only a moment. In the dim light of the lamp. One small pool in the blackness. It was like a mask. White with a slash of orange on her mouth and two slashes of black to mark her eyes. She was looking at me but she did not see me. Then the mask was down again and the light illuminated nothing but the top of her head. That thick auburn hair.

I stepped back behind the door. I stayed pressed against the wall, not wanting to go back into the kitchen and not wanting to go to my room.

*Do you want to tell me what happened?*

*Frances*, she said, and it was all she said.

He was silent. The slow soothing words had been abruptly cut and in their stead there was only silence. Awful, heavy silence until finally he spoke again. But his voice was not what it was. It was cracked and uncertain.

*What has happened?*

It was Dorothy speaking now, cutting over him. *She has gone*, and her voice was flat and thin.

And that was when I looked again. I remember, looking around the door because I did not know what was going on, and I saw him and I did not understand.

He looked . . . I cannot think of the word.

Shattered.

He looked shattered.

I did not understand.

I still do not understand.

I remember all this, as I plant the herbs, one by one, concentrating on the ground in front of me, while John Mills talks to me.

*I want to*, he says, *I want to explain,* and I decide I will put all the herbs here in this bed, all in a row.

The flowers I will leave for the back fence. I want them to grow tall. I want them to hide us from the road. I want them to hide us from everyone who walks past, from everyone who has ever pointed or stared, from everyone who knows.

# 39

I could not explain.

When I first told Martin about Frances that night at Marissa and Robert's, he had asked me how I could bear it. *Not knowing.*

And he had sat up in bed and wanted to write his list. He had wanted to solve it. This is the way he is. For Martin there is always an explanation.

I tried to tell him I had been over everything. Over and over. With them and by myself, tracing and retracing that day and then the day before that and the one before that and every day I could remember, so that on bad days they all became one and I felt I did not know anything.

I tried to tell him I had envisaged it all, the worst I could imagine and the best.

Frances under the jetty where the Coke cans and cigarette butts bob up and down, up and down on the slippery surface of the sea, thick foam curling around her toes while they held her down, held her under. The boys on the jetty, peeling off their skin-tight jeans, the man in the kiosk, and I would see his long fingernails. I would see things I could not bear to see. I would see him, too. I would see John Mills and I would see those photographs and I would not know what it was I was seeing. I would wake up and I would remember. I would see her on a bus going somewhere, somewhere far away from here, and I would breathe again. It was all right. She had gone but it was all right. And from the next room, I would hear her, Dorothy. Clipping and pasting, clipping and pasting. 'Similar Stories' and 'Possibilities' piled high around us.

I tried to tell him this but I did not have the words.

He was sitting up in bed. There had to be a way we could work it out. If we went over every detail. Wrote a list. *How can you bear it?*

You begin by searching for a defined event and you find you are searching for something larger. You are trying to understand it all. One life and then the lives that connect with that life, and there is no end. There is no list that could encompass it all.

How could I explain?

For Martin, there are only defined events. He would not have understood. He will never understand.

That night was the only time he and I spoke of Frances. He was, I suppose, uncomfortable. He was, I suppose, frightened of how I would react.

I was used to being silent.

But sometimes I wished he would speak. I wished he

would just ask me something, anything, so that I could talk of her. I would wait for him to mention her name. I would hope he would mention her name.

But he never did.

And sometimes I hated him for that silence.

In my mother's back yard now, John Mills waits for me to turn and look at him.

*How can I explain?* He leans forward to see my face. I do not want him to know that I am anxious he is about to admit something I do not want to hear, something that makes no sense. Because he is a good man. A part of me knows that. A part of me has always known it and that is why I have never really understood why he had those photographs.

*It is not what you think it is,* he tells me. *It is not what you think it is.*

And as he tries to talk to me, I am, at first, afraid. I am afraid that he is going to pull all that I have tried to understand back into a single event, that he is going to tell me that there was a defining moment I had missed all those years ago. Something I had failed to see as I lay in my rock pool, my back to the jetty, unaware of what was occurring around me. And I am not sure if I can bear to have it revealed to me.

But he doesn't.

It is not that day he is talking about. It is not even that summer he is talking about. It is something else. It is another time.

And as he tries to tell me, I do not know how I could not have known. I do not know how I could have failed to see what I know he is trying to explain to me, not just on that day, but on the days before that, and the days after that, and every single day that I had thought about my sister.

Because there was something I had missed. He is trying to explain. He is trying to tell me about her. And with his first words, I know what he is wanting to say, and this is what I cannot bear. To know, and in knowing, having to grapple with how I had spent so long not knowing.

My mother would hold her arms out wide, *He loved me, this much, he loved me, he loved me, he loved me . . .* while my sister would look on. She would look on, and in her eyes there would be scorn. Anger, contempt and scorn. And in her voice there would be mockery, sneering as she would repeat my mother's words, over and over again.

I do not know how I could not have known.

*I need to tell you*, he says, and he speaks softly; he does not want to say this any louder, but with me by the garden bed, concentrating on making each row straight, he is forced to speak up.

*Do you remember,* he asks me, *when your father came home? In that year before he died?*

I remember, but I do not know what I remember.

I can feel the sun on the back of my neck. I can feel an ant, crawling from my wrist into the sleeve of my shirt.

I remember but I do not know what I remember.

And he is holding a file out towards me. *She was only eight.*

I lay the spade down at my feet. He is looking at me, looking straight at me, wanting me to take it from him, wanting me to hear what it is he has to say. And I am surprised at how aged his hands are. White, frail, shaking, as I take the folder from him and step back, back to where I had been standing, by the border of pebbles, smooth and pale under the sun.

I do not want to read what is in my hands. I do not want to see. I do not want to listen. I do not want to know.

My sister. There in his surgery, with Dorothy next to her, and as I read his report, *difficulty urinating, unwilling to be examined,* he is talking to me, he is telling me. His notes, his words there on the page, *a bike accident,* and his words now.

*You must understand, at the time we knew very little about cases like this. Now, if I were still a doctor, I would have no hesitation in taking it further.* All he is saying floats around me and I cannot bring myself to look at him. I cannot bring myself to see what I know I will see.

It was so long ago. I do not know why he is telling me this.

I do not know what he wants me to say.

I do not want to hear what I know I am hearing.

But I keep seeing my sister, I keep seeing her and I am forced to listen. I am forced to listen to all she tried to say. *He didn't love her, he just wanted to stick it into her.* And she rolls her eyes in disgust. She rolls her eyes and she dances round and round the room. *He loved me, he loved me, he loved me, helovedme, helovedme,*

228

*helovedmehelovedmehelovedmehelovedme*, rolling her eyes and hitching her skirt up, up, up, up, and I want to tell her to shut up, to just shut up, but she doesn't, she won't, she wouldn't.

He loved me. This much.

The paper is dry in my hands. I close the folder slowly and do not know what to do with it. The cardboard is creased, bent at the spine, worn from where it has been opened and folded back. The pages inside have yellowed. Covered in faded blue ink. Words that say nothing.

*She came back*, John Mills tells me, *to see me. Three weeks later, on her own*. His hands rest on his inner thighs. The knuckles are white.

*I tried to talk to her*. His head is bent, low.

I am laying the file down on the ground and I am looking at him. I am watching him as he struggles for his words. *I did nothing*. It is all he can manage to say.

On the day we learnt that my father died, my sister cried. It was the only time I saw her in tears. I am listening to him and I am remembering. *I did it,* she tells me. *I did it because I wanted it. I wanted him dead*. I am hearing her words and I am hearing his words, John Mills trying to say what he needs to say. Trying to explain that this is what he has lived with, knowing but not wanting to know. Hoping that it was not what he thought it was, trying to see, there, in my sister's face, that she was all right, that it was just a bike accident, nothing else. Needing to get closer, to convince himself that it was not as he knew it was, holding his photographs under the light, laying them out on the table, trying to reassure himself.

Just as I have been doing.

He loved me. This much.

I do not know how I could not have known.

I look out across the yard, past the back fence and to the streets beyond and I am seeing it all as a stranger would see it.

*Did she know?* I ask him, and I turn my head back in the direction of the house, back in the direction of my mother's bedroom.

*I don't know.*

*Was it him?*

He shakes his head. *I don't know. It might have been. But I don't know. It could have been anyone.*

It could have been anyone.

And I see them all. The boys on the jetty. Jim Hunt at the kiosk. My father.

*I have to talk to her,* I tell him. *I have to speak to her*, and he reaches to stop me as I pass him, but I do not let him.

# 40

I have told my story. Over and over again.

I have told it in its entirety and I have told it in parts.

*That bit again, please,* and I oblige.

I can say it forwards, I can say it backwards, and I can say it inside out. I can tell it to them and I can tell it to myself. I can go into every detail or I can tell it briefly, the salient facts, the eyeteeth, the important parts . . .

I have told my story.

Once upon a time, a long time ago, there were two little girls. Frances and Elise.

More times than I could begin to count.

Once upon a time, a long time ago, there were two little girls. Frances and Elise. They lived in a suburb by the beach. A suburb where the roads stretched long and straight and flat from east to west and from north to south, and where the houses sprawled, one after the other after the other.

In the summer it was hot. Long dry days that scorched the back yards and the small strips of grass by the footpath, burning them into the dirt. The trees sagged and sighed in the heat, and everyone kept their blinds drawn and their doors closed, trying to trap what little cool there was in shaded dusty living rooms.

In the winter, the winds and the rain came, and it was cold. The winds crept in through every crack, under windows, under doors, and they brought the damp and the salt with them. The sea heaved, dark and furious, dragging seaweed up from its slimy depths and throwing it across the cold grey sand.

This was the place where Frances and Elise lived. A long time ago. They knew the streets, and the shops, and the road that led down to the beach, and the dunes, and the miles of sand that stretched long and straight, and the sea, and the jetties, one on this beach, one on the next and one on the beach after that.

In the summer holidays they went down to the ocean. Every day. Walking down the same stretch of road, stopping at the same place near the kiosk to confer briefly, and then they spent the day apart until they came home together, back up the same path, past the kiosk again, and along the same straight flat roads that led to home.

This was the way it was. Each day the same, harsh blue sky, hot white sand, sunburnt noses and small petty fights, over and over.

This was the way it was, until that day.

The day that it happened.

The day that Elise went home alone.

And from then on, she was told to distinguish that day from all the other days because they thought that if she could do that, if she could find that difference, then they would know, they would know. And so she tried. Over and over and over. Tracing and retracing each step, each look, each word. And she knew each element that she sifted. She knew the fights that they had in the morning, she knew the way they walked, she knew the words they spoke to each other before they separated; she knew all those ingredients. But in all her years of sifting she had not known, she had never really known, the central element, Frances.

Frances.

And in the seaside suburb that was their home, the police were also searching. They, too, were sifting through each fact that was presented to them. Up and down that beach, in the burning heat, sifting through each grain of sand, and out on the ocean, using helicopters and boats, looking above and below.

And they questioned; they questioned neighbours and shop owners, and friends and family, over and over until they pieced together a picture, a broad picture. They knew what she looked like, they knew who her friends were, they knew what she did, but they did not know, they did not really know, who she was.

*Hate to say it, but that's what happens to girls like her,* and they would all snicker.

Girls like her.

Over the back fences, they would shake their heads in disapproval, or look at each other knowingly. Washing flapping, clean against a blank morning sky, as they would catch up on the latest news: *Did you hear they've been questioning Terry's kids? Nothing serious, just routine.*

*Hate to say it, but I always thought that girl would come to no good.*

And they would thank the heavens their kids weren't like that.

In the classroom, the bell would ring, sharp and jarring, and they would slam their books shut and run out into the yard where they would gather in their various groups. Under the shade of the tea-trees, out on the oval, skirts hitched up to the thighs, by the canteen or in the airconditioned cool of the library.

*My mum says she had it coming to her,* and they would all look at Jo-anne or Diane or Lisa and nod their heads in agreement.

*You look like you're asking for it and you're gonna get it. Sooner or later,* and they would all nod again.

*Police reckon she was raped. Probably by a whole gang,* and there would be a moment's silence.

*Well, you know she'd already done it?* Disbelief on all their faces.

*True. Johnno's sister, Kerry, told me that most of those boys had done it with her.*

So it would go. Over and over and over. Throughout that summer and into the winter, dragging on, the full force of its momentum gradually dying until it was reduced to just a few small scraps, the occasional word, rekindled haphazardly and then burning out again because they had picked it bare. All of them. Picked it to its bones without ever knowing, really knowing, who she was.

And I stand now, in the doorway of my mother's room, looking at it all and feeling like I no longer know it. Any of it. Because all I have held to be familiar can no longer be trusted. It has to be seen differently now. It has to be, and I walk in without knocking.

# 41

My father sits in a picture frame by my mother's bed. This photograph and her words are all I really know of him. When I try to see him as he was when he was home, I can only see his face as it is behind that glass. When I try to hear the words he would have spoken, I can only hear her words.

*What was he like?* Martin once asked me.

I told him I did not know.

Dorothy lies flat on her back, her newspapers strewn across the blankets. Her eyes are closed but I doubt she is asleep. Her breakfast tray rests on the empty space next to her, an empty cup of black coffee, strong, the way my father liked it, and a leftover corner of toast.

I pick it up and put it on the bedside table, near that picture.

*I do not remember him,* I told Martin. *I was only four when he died.*

I hold the photograph under the light, wanting to see his face, but in its brightness, there is only reflection.

Dorothy moves. I see her shifting. I see her wanting to know what it is I am doing but not opening her eyes.

I wipe the dust from the glass and tilt the frame away from the light. This is the face of the man who is my father. This is the face of the man who met my mother, down under the jetty, and in the darkness, pressed her up against the pylon, out of sight of the others, out of hearing. My mother has told me this. I know this. But I do not know why I always felt that there was more. Drunk on whisky with her body crushed by his, she did not know how to stop something she did not understand.

*He married her because she was pregnant. Because he had to*, Frances would whisper. But did she ever whisper more than that? There are things I sense. I know her words and I know Dorothy's words. I know what those words say and what they do not say.

My mother opens her eyes. One blue, one green. The sky and the trees. Or was it the lakes and the trees? I do not remember.

She is looking at me, watching me as I put the photograph back in its place, leaning it up against the wall where it has always sat.

My hands are shaking.

Where do I begin?

In the silence of this room, in the silence of this house, you could hear a pin drop, you could hear a breath of wind from off the ocean, you could hear the next-door neighbour slamming the back door shut behind her, and you can hear her now, out the back, her voice carrying down the side of the house and into my mother's open window as she tells him, John Mills, that it looks like winter is over. *Finally*, she says.

*I know*, he answers, *it's a beautiful day*, and his words are clear, loud and clear, in this room.

My mother does not take her eyes from my face.

*You heard?* I ask her and she does not blink. *You heard us? John and me? Before?*

Outside they continue to talk. *How is she?* the next-door neighbour asks him, and he tells her she's on the mend. *It won't be long before she's up on her feet*, he says.

Dorothy coughs.

*You must speak to me*, I say. *You have to talk to me,* and I am reaching for the photograph again, but she stops me, her hand cool and dry on mine.

*Don't*, she says and it is all she says.

In the darkness of this room, I can just see the two of us. There, reflected in the mirror on her dressing-table. I cannot see our faces, only my torso and, there, on the bed, the shape that I know is my mother, her hand out-stretched to mine, both of us reaching for him. My father.

I let my arm fall.

My father worked on the lines, out where the scrub lies low and flat and the soil slips dry like sand through your fingers.

*He did not want to leave me,* and Dorothy would sigh, *but we had no money. It is a testament to our love. Because he did love me. This much,* and she would stretch her arms out wide, or was it Frances who did that? I do not know.

My father came home when he was between jobs. A week here, a few days there, and in the year he died, he was back for a couple of months.

If I try to remember him from this time, I have only a sense of his presence. I have no solid memories, no incidents that I can recall; *I was only four*, I told Martin, *my recollections are vague*. I have nothing but a sense; a sense from years of stumbling in the dark. This is all I can rely upon.

*Did he do it?* I ask my mother, finally finding the words I want, but as I speak, I know there is no point. She speaks in stories, one piled on top of the other. Any truth that once existed has long since been buried, so dark so deep so forgotten, rotten at the bottom of the pile.

She looks at me and she looks beyond me.

*We loved each other, your father and I, really loved each other*, and she wipes her hair back from her face, her beautiful hair, the envy of all the other girls, as she talks of him, the same words over and over again.

She reaches for my hand and I am about to pull away, I am about to turn from her, but then I see us both again, there in the mirror, just the two of us, her lying in her bed and me standing by her side.

There is only her and me. This is what is left. And she will have no answers for me. Not if I shook her, not if I shouted at her, not if I begged or pleaded.

*She was only eight*, I say, but I am saying it to myself.

*Please, sit with me*, she asks, and I do not move.

*Please*, she asks again, and I find that I cannot.

I am turning my back on her and I am walking out of

her room and out of this house. I do not know where I want to go. I just know that I have to get out, and I push the front door with the entire weight of my body so that when it opens, I am catapulted out on to the verandah, squinting in the brightness of the last of the day.

*My sister,* I whisper to the first tint of pink in the sky. *My sister.*

My voice is louder now; loud and clear across our yard, over the road and behind me, back into our house.

*My sister was not what you thought she was.*

I am telling myself, I am telling her and I am telling the world. Because it has to be said. Out loud.

*My sister was not what you thought she was.*

And my voice is shaky, but it is strong.

I walk down our steps and along the road. I have my back to the sea and I am walking away from it. But I could just as easily be walking in the other direction, towards that stretch of sand, towards that jetty, and far out, the old men fishing, there at the end.

And I remember. It was Frances who had told me that they fish for sharks. I had accepted what she had said but I had never really believed her. I hadn't wanted to think that they were out there. Not that close to shore.

But I should have listened. It seems she was right.

And I want to tell her that I am sorry.

I want to tell her that I should have listened.

But all I can do is repeat those words, over and over again. *My sister was not what you thought she was.* Chanting them to myself as I walk with my back to the sea.

# 42

When I first moved in with Martin, I rang my mother twice a day. In the morning and in the evening.

*It's a bit excessive, isn't it?* Martin used to say.

He thought I was overly concerned about her. *She's a survivor,* he would tell me. *Tougher than she looks.*

He did not understand that it was not just concern that made me call.

I missed her. In a way I could not explain.

Because when you have lived with someone for a long time, just the two of you, it is not so easy to leave the other behind. It is not so easy to turn your back and walk away. Even when it is what you want.

My mother and I lived in this house, just the two of us, for fourteen years.

There was no one else.

We did not have a lot to say to each other. Our acknowledgement of each other's presence was infrequent and insubstantial, but that is not to say that we were not enmeshed. We could not help but be. We only had each other.

So, when I left her, I could not leave her.

I am bound to her. Even when she fails me.

I sit in my mother's kitchen and from the other room I can hear John Mills reading to her. I can hear his voice, going over each of the stories in each of the papers, and I put my head in my hands, not wanting to listen.

*I am sorry*, he said when I came home yesterday afternoon and found him still waiting.

I did not want to talk to him about it. Not then.

Today when he arrived I was in the garden finishing the last of the planting. He wanted to speak. I could see it in his face. But still I could not find the words and, again, he knew.

*I'll just go and see how she is,* he said, leaving me as I wanted to be left. Alone.

He was still in Dorothy's room when I came inside and I could hear her, dictating to him, her endless letters to others with a similar story. And when she finished, she asked him if he would mind reading just a few articles to her, only one or two, before he left.

This is my mother.

I put my head in my hands and I close my eyes, not wanting to hear.

This is my mother.

I am bound to her, but this is not the place to which I have to return.

I have arranged to meet Jocelyn at her house after

work, and when I arrive, she tells me I am doing the right thing. *It feels terrible at the time,* she reassures me, *but you will soon wonder why you didn't do it earlier.*

She drives us both up the long road that leads to Martin's mother's house. We do not talk. I stare out the window, looking at the houses I know so well, and remember the day when he drove me here, all that I owned in the boot of his car.

*It will be all right*, he had reassured me when he had seen that I was thinking about her, Dorothy, alone in that house. *You will soon wonder why you didn't do it earlier*, and he had patted me on the leg and told me to cheer up.

When we pull into the drive, the house looks like a house I do not know. But then this is how it has always seemed. It has never been my place. It has always been Martin's mother's house.

There are leaves on the path that leads up through the neatly clipped lawn to the entrance. The next-door neighbour's dog has been at the hose again, and I know that Martin will swear loudly when he sees where it has been chewed.

*Jesus Christ*, he will say, as he comes stomping through the front door, being careful to first wipe his feet on the mat. *It's about time she did something about that animal*, and his words will echo unanswered down the hush of the carpeted hall. But then this is how it has always been. I gave up answering him a long time ago; hearing him, but not hearing him.

Jocelyn waits for me in her car while I let myself in. All the blinds are drawn and it is dark inside.

My few clothes are in the wardrobe, my shoes in a neat row on the floor. In the spare room, my box is unopened at the back of the cupboard, as I left it all those years ago.

I am about to leave, I am about to close the door behind me, when I realise I have forgotten something. For a moment, I cannot think where I put it, and then I remember. I left it in the laundry, the blue satin nightgown that Dorothy gave me for my twenty-eighth birthday.

The clothes-horse is folded and stacked by the door. The bucket in which I tried to soak the stains out of the material has been put back under the sink.

For a moment I am at a loss as to where to look, but it is only for a moment.

I know Martin. I know him well, and I open the cupboard and take out the rag bag, Dorothy's nightgown shining silver-blue on top.

It is slippery smooth beneath my fingers.

I shake it out and let it run, like water, over my arms and into my bag of clothes.

*That's all?* Jocelyn asks me when I come out to where she is waiting for me.

*That's all*, I tell her.

She turns the car in the cul-de-sac at the end of this street and I do not look back as we drive off, away from the house that I had once hoped would be my escape and back down the road I know so well. The road that leads to my mother's.

*Are you all right?* Jocelyn asks me as she drops me off.

I tell her that I am fine.

I stack my things in the hall, knowing that Dorothy will see them when she is well enough to walk. They are stacked by the door. Soon she will see them and she will see that I am not going to stay.

*Where will you go?* Martin asks me on the telephone. *Back to Dot's?*

I tell Martin I do not know my plans. I do not know where I will go.

He says he has started seeing someone else. He tells me he wanted me to find out from him. He hopes it will not affect our work relationship.

I do not know what to say.

I look at the keys to his mother's house, still on my key ring, and I wonder how long it will be before he gives them to her. Not long. I cannot imagine Martin by himself for long. But I do not want to think about it. Not yet.

# 43

It takes about three weeks for a fracture like my mother's to heal enough to be able to walk and, as she leans on my arm, we make our way, carefully, step by step, into the yard.

I have not told her about the garden, but I know she knows. Just as she heard John and me speaking that morning two weeks ago, she would have also heard us discuss this, the rows of lettuces and herbs along the side, and by the back gate, the flowers and corn that will soon grow high enough to cover the fence. But she has not said a word. And nor have I. This is the way it is. This is the way it has always been and this is the way it will probably stay. There are no miraculous changes, just slow steps forward, inch by inch.

In the bright sunlight, Dorothy squints. I show her each of the plants and she does not speak.

*These*, I tell her, *are foxgloves. And these*, I reach to touch the tiny leaves, *are sunflowers.*

*The pigface has gone?* she finally asks me.

I tell her that it has.

*It was not so bad*, she says, and she looks around her.

I do not know if she likes what she sees. If she did, it is unlikely she would tell me.

*And who will look after all this?* she asks.

When I tell her that she will have to, she shrugs again.

*I guessed as much*, she says and turns back towards the house.

I have arranged to meet John this morning. I want to talk about how we can care for her. But this is not all. He sits with Dorothy during the day, arriving after I have left for work and leaving when I come home. We pass each other. Speaking briefly about her health, a few words at the back gate under the darkness of the evening sky. He has tried, once or twice, to lead me back to what was said. He has tried and I have not yet followed. Eyes down, the gate closed, telling him I would see him tomorrow.

*Not yet*, I wanted to say, but I could not even say those words. Not yet.

The street is empty. There is a cool breeze from off the ocean and the more slender of the branches overhead lift and fall, lift and fall, slow and distant. On the path to the beach the grasses would be swaying, the ripple of a cloth as it settles, and the sand and the sea would be sparkling sharp and clear under the stark blue of this sky.

John Mills is in his back garden. I see his head over the fence and I knock, once, on the high wooden gate, before letting myself in.

This is what I see first. Him, and beyond that the back

door where I once knocked loud enough to wake the dead. I do not see what lies at my feet. I do not see it in all its splendour until I am standing on it, and the dazzle of the colour that surrounds me is overwhelming.

*I have finished*, he tells me.

It is beautiful. Eyes of china blue, each iris the size of a fist, each lash coal black, cheeks of eggshell, hair that tumbles gold and red, and in her hand a single flower, open wide, showing its face to the world. The colours dance, they glitter and dance, alive before me, sparkling in the early morning sun.

I look up at him and I can see the delight in his face. *I never thought I would*, he tells me. *But I have.*

He has, and it is more than I had ever envisioned.

*It is beautiful*, I say, my voice quiet in the stillness. *Just beautiful.*

We sit at the table and we are awkward.

*I am sorry*, he says again. *So sorry*, and I know he is and I know he does not know what else to say. *I wanted to give you these*, and I take the envelope. *If you don't want them, I will understand.*

I know what they are before I open them. I can feel them beneath my fingers and I take them out, all of them, holding them in my hand. I want to ask him if he thinks she might have run away, got on a bus and just gone, unable to cope with all that was never said, turning her back on us, all of us, but I do not say those words out loud. He does not know. I do not know. We will probably never know, and I lay the prints out, one by one, across the table.

This is my sister.

This is Frances.

And at the end I put my photo next to her. I take it out from my bag, and I lay it down with the others.

Two young girls. Awkward, thin and misplaced.

**Little White Secrets**   Catherine Jinks

*Gossip, gossip, gossip. Alice had been fending off inquiries for days: it was out in the open now, with a vengeance. People were talking about David all over town . . .*

David French leaves Sydney to work in Sable Cove, a small Canadian fishing town, convinced that a year away from his lover will repair their failing relationship. But he's not prepared for life in a community where everyone has something to hide – and where it's always a fight to keep your secrets to yourself.

At once poignant and entertaining, and full of the razor-sharp perception that has become Catherine Jinks's signature, *Little White Secrets* takes us behind the facade of a place that isn't quite what it seems.

'As an eloquent storyteller, as queen of the narrative drive, Catherine Jinks is filling a void in Australian literature. Like Joanna Trollope and Mary Wesley she finds drama in the complicated lives of modern families . . . '
Dianne Dempsey, *The Sunday Age*

**Swallowing Clouds**    Lillian Ng

In a vivid past life in ancient China, Syn was drowned in a pig's basket for committing adultery. Now a soothsayer warns that she will never find happiness in love.

When Syn journeys from Old Shanghai to the streets of modern Sydney and becomes entangled in a steamy and dangerous affair with Zhu, history threatens to repeat itself. Troubled by her past, a woman in the grip of passion, Syn is also full of hope for the future.

Seductive and poignant, rich with Oriental tales and superstitions, *Swallowing Clouds* explores the limits of love and history.

### Unseemly Longing  Margaret Geddes

*'You must wonder why this has happened to you,' someone said when I was in hospital. I didn't. I don't. It was clear from the moment I opened my eyes in intensive care that the question is 'Why not?' This is a random game of roulette we're playing, and we don't get to spin the chamber.*

Kirsten Campbell has confronted the ultimate experience. Now, trapped between a detachment from life and a longing for death, she is given a second chance . . .

A courageous and unflinching novel about who people are – and who they might be.

**Lovesong**   Elizabeth Jolley

*Miss Vales: I never ever clap eyes on him.*

*Mrs Porter: Well, he's around all right, EV, coming and going all day he is – up and down the stairs, in and out the whole day long and half the night . . .*

To Mrs Porter's establishment – a Home away from Home for Homeless Gentlemen – comes Dalton Foster, recently and reluctantly returning to the community. Dalton is intent on a fresh start. So is Miss Emily Vales, fellow lodger, and recipient of Mrs Porter's tea-leaves predictions . . .

Across the park from Dalton's cold, bleak room is the large, overdraped house of his childhood, where now another Consul's family lives. Intrigued and well-meaning, they welcome him into the house, unaware of Dalton's past links – and his yearnings.

'Love at its most desperate, lit by flashes of Jolley's wild humour, and sweetened by her patient tenderness.'

Helen Garner